Dear Reader,

A few days ago I got a letter from a certain J. D. Mallory, biologist and wolf expert, saying that "the below signed" would be joining me on my assignment for *Preservation* magazine. Jessica Mallory, I thought to myself, what kind of games are you playing?

Doesn't she think I remember her? I mean, how could I forget that kiss—it made my head spin. At sixteen, she was way too young, but believe me, it took all my strength to keep my hands off her.

Now she's all grown-up—and still playing hide-and-seek? What could she *possibly* be afraid of? That the chemistry's still there? That she might actually forgive me for breaking her heart?

Hey, as I see it, she wouldn't have agreed to come if she didn't want to find out. And she *will* find out.

Ben Standish

ANNE McALLISTER

To Tame a Wolf

Michigan

Harlequin Books

TORONTO • NEW YORK • LONDON
AMSTERDAM • PARIS • SYDNEY • HAMBURG
STOCKHOLM • ATHENS • TOKYO • MILAN
MADRID • WARSAW • BUDAPEST • AUCKLAND

To Patrick.
I couldn't have done it without you.

HARLEQUIN ENTERPRISES LTD.
225 Duncan Mill Road, Don Mills,
Ontario, Canada M3B 3K9

TO TAME A WOLF

Copyright © 1987 by Barbara Schenck

All rights reserved. Except for use in any review, the reproduction
or utilization of this work in whole or in part in any form by any
electronic, mechanical or other means, now known or hereafter
invented, including xerography, photocopying and recording, or in
any information storage or retrieval system, is forbidden without
the permission of the publisher, Harlequin Enterprises Ltd.,
225 Duncan Mill Road, Don Mills, Ontario, Canada M3B 3K9

ISBN: 0-373-45172-5

Published Harlequin Enterprises, Ltd. 1987, 1993

All the characters in this book have no existence outside the
imagination of the author and have no relation whatsoever to
anyone bearing the same name or names. They are not even
distantly inspired by any individual known or unknown to the
author, and all incidents are pure invention.

® and ™ are trademarks used under license. Trademarks recorded
with ® are registered in the United States Patent and Trademark
Office, the Canadian Trade Marks Office and in other countries.

Printed in the U.S.A.

CHAPTER ONE

SHE WOULD have known Ben Standish anywhere.

He hadn't changed a bit.

He was just as lean, dark and dangerous-looking as he had ever been. Exactly the sort of man who ought to be labelled injurious to the heart.

Well, he wasn't going to injure her heart. Not again, Jessica Mallory thought, shifting the heavy backpack on her shoulders and crossing the tarmac towards the air terminal where she could see him lounging against the glass. After the job he had done on her eight years ago, there was no way she would fall for him this time.

All the same, she was glad she had known ahead of time just whom she was going to be up against. She had had two weeks to prepare herself for spending these two and a half weeks in White Birch Bay with him, while he wrote and photographed an article for *Preservation* magazine on the biological study being done in that remote upper peninsula Michigan area prior to possible developments. He, on the other hand, only knew that the biologist he was going with

was the wolf expert, J.D. Mallory. It was all she had
told him in the terse professional memo she had sent
him. It wasn't exactly a lie, but it wasn't the whole
truth either. Jessica didn't care. She didn't owe him
that.

The muggy mid-July heat made her perspire on
just the short walk across the airfield. It had to be
that which made her palms damp and her shirt stick
to her sides. It had to be that which made her face
hot and moist.

It couldn't be Ben Standish!

She brushed her long blonde hair back out of her
face and drew a deep breath. Then she pushed open
the door to the air terminal and walked straight towards him. He was standing just inside the glass
doors now, less than ten feet from her. And though
it had been eight years since she had seen him, it
might have been only last night.

He was slightly more filled out now than she remembered him being at twenty-four. But he was still
lean and rangy. Dark shaggy hair fell across his
forehead with the same casual grace it always had.
And he was obviously still given to wearing snug blue
jeans and plaid cotton shirts with the sleeves rolled
back on his forearms. But although her quick pe-
rusal took in all these things about him, registering
them in the back of her mind, she was really focusing on his eyes.

More than anything else she remembered Ben Standish's eyes. Tawny eyes, flecked with gold and green. Wolf's eyes, she thought now. And although she told herself that was fanciful, she knew, in fact, that it was not. She had see a lot of wolves over the past few years, and she was struck now by how closely Ben's eyes resembled theirs. It was uncanny, unnerving, and exactly what she didn't want to think about. She had a weakness for wolves; she didn't want any weakness where Ben was concerned.

Because the other thing she realised immediately was that her physical attraction to him hadn't changed either. It was sharp, instantaneous, and close to overwhelming. She wanted desperately to turn tail and run.

But she was an adult now, she reminded herself, not an impressionable teenage girl. And this man had betrayed her. That alone ought to help her keep her raging hormones under control. And a split second's reflection on it did just that.

She held out her hand to the dark-haired man who closed the distance between them and said coolly, 'Mr Standish?'

It was possible, even likely, that he would be shocked to discover that J.D. Mallory was a woman.

But she didn't see shock on his face. Instead a small smile twitched the corner of his mouth as his rough, calloused hand enveloped hers. 'Jess.'

She stared. 'You—you *knew?*' she accused, unable to keep the dismay out of her voice. It was obvious that he had known, and was now enjoying her discomfiture. She started to seethe.

'Of course I knew.'

'But—'

He grinned, unrepentant. 'I always make it a point to get to know the people I'm going to be working with.'

'That's right, you do,' Jess said bitterly, remembering just how well Ben had got to know her mother eight years ago. She tried to pull her hand out of his grasp, but he hung on.

'You're looking beautiful,' he told her, ignoring her barbed comment. 'Quite a lot like your mother, actually.'

Jess did manage to jerk her hand away then. How dared he?

It was true, what he had said, and she knew it. But she didn't like being reminded. Her teenage coltishness had softened. Her angles had become curves, though they were more modest than her mother's.

But then, Jess thought waspishly, everything about her was more modest than Clarissa. Still, the resemblance was strong. She had turned out remarkably like her mother. Most people didn't know that the famous actress Clarissa Evans was Jessica's mother. But even the ones who didn't often told her she reminded them of a movie star, though frequently they didn't know which.

Ben Standish, however, knew exactly which and, all things considered, Jess thought it was the height of tactlessness for him to bring it up.

'I am not at all like my mother,' she told him sharply.

'I see.' His tone was non-committal, and the way he looked at her made Jess wonder what it was he thought he saw. She had another strong urge to turn around and jump back on the plane to Madison, leaving Ben Standish behind.

But if she did that, she would be leaving her job behind, too. Over the past two weeks Gunnar Halvorsen, her boss at the Natural Resource Research Institute, had taken great pains to instruct her how to be cordial to Ben Standish. He had stressed how many of Ben's readers would be in a position to contribute to NRRI's research funds, and that she should be careful not to alienate him.

And she had assured Gunnar that she would be the epitome of professionalism. So she stood her ground, swallowing all the retorts she felt like making, forcing herself to think of Ben as a journalist and nothing but. It was the only way she was going to make it, she realised.

'Where's the transport you said you'd provide?' she asked him, wanting to get started.

'Just outside in the lot. We can go as soon as you get your gear.' He headed for the baggage claim area, but Jess stopped him.

'I have everything in my pack. I always travel light. It's best that way.'

Ben surveyed her jeans-clad figure carefully as if he were checking out her backpack. In fact, Jess knew he was doing nothing of the sort. His eyes barely glanced at the grey nylon pack on her shoulders. Instead they roved down over her breasts and hips, then worked their way back up her slim figure, lingering on her bosom which jutted out against her blue chambray shirt because of the weight of the pack on her back. Then, after a careful examination that made her hot all over, they moved upward to study her face, noting the wide mouth, the uptilted nose with its spattering of freckles, and the eyes that she had finally grown into.

Jess felt her cheeks burn under his scrutiny, and she glared at him. But he didn't seem to take the hint.

Finally, leisurely, he reached out and adjusted the strap on her left shoulder. 'Nice,' he mused, but the tilt of his grin and the spark of teasing fire she saw in his tawny eyes told her he wasn't talking about the pack.

'The transport, Mr Standish,' she prodded.

'Right.' He turned on his heel and headed for the small car park just on the far side of the air terminal.

Jess followed, still feeling the touch of his fingers against her shoulder, hating how intensely she was aware of him, telling herself it was wrong, foolish, and any number of other things at the same time that her eyes feasted on him as he walked.

She had always liked to watch the way Ben moved. He had the sort of lithe, compact grace that she admired. He was wolf-like in that respect too, she thought. It was too bad he had inherited none of their finer characteristics such as commitment, fidelity, loyalty.

His shoulders flexed easily beneath the soft cotton of his madras shirt as he pushed the door open and held it while she passed. Jess deliberately looked away from him, forcing her thoughts in another direction.

Which of the trucks in the car park was his? she wondered. She was astounded when he stopped suddenly next to a good-sized camper.

'This?' Her shock was obvious in her voice.

'Home sweet home.'

'Not *my* home,' she said abruptly, having a very clear idea of where this conversation was about to lead.

'No,' said Ben, unlatching the door. 'Mine. Yours temporarily.'

'Not mine at all. Ever. Period.'

'Why not?'

He seemed to be asking with total indifference, as if he couldn't begin to comprehend why she would object to sharing a camper with him.

'Because—' Jess began, but stopped suddenly because she remembered Gunnar's admonishments, and everything she was about to say sounded inane and missish and unprofessional to boot. Her mouth opened and closed like a fish.

In the meantime, Ben swung open the door. 'Just take a look.'

Jess didn't want to look. Her mind was whirling at the rate of a million miles a minute. Ben Standish was a walking approach-avoidance conflict as far as she was concerned. She sensed that the minute she saw him again. All her common sense had gone flying right out the window. And she didn't want to be in a camper with him at all.

She wanted a quick trip to a motel. She wanted separate rooms for the night. And when they packed into White Birch Bay, she wanted separate tents. She didn't want this kind of proximity. Not at all.

'I'll rent a car,' she said.

Before Ben could protest she had spun on her heel and headed back towards the terminal. She half expected he would follow her, but he didn't, thank heavens! She felt an enormous relief—until the man behind the car rental counter said, 'Sorry, we're all out.'

'All out?' echoed Jess, unable to believe her ears.

He spread his hands. 'We only got half a dozen, lady. Last Wednesday we had some fellas fly in from Chicago, and they took 'em to go fishing for three weeks.'

Jess rubbed a hand through her hair and sighed. Not one car? The pack was cutting into her shoulders. It was all this standing around that was doing it. If she were hiking, moving easily and at a steady pace, she wouldn't even notice it. She glanced around the terminal, half hoping to see some solution to her problem. All she saw, out of the corner of her eye, was Ben, still leaning nonchalantly against the side of his camper and watching her. She gritted her teeth.

'When do you expect one of your cars back?'

'Like I told you. Two and a half weeks, probably. May get one sooner, but I couldn't guarantee it.'

'Damn,' she muttered under her breath. 'Is there any other place nearby to rent one?'

He shook his head. 'This ain't Chicago, lady.'

It certainly wasn't. And most times Jess would have rather been in upper peninsula Michigan than in any urban metropolis on earth. But she didn't feel that way right now.

She chewed on her lip, contemplating her next move. There wasn't much question about what it would have to be. She would have to turn around and walk about back out to the camper and go with Ben Standish.

'Damn,' she said again. 'Damn, damn, damn!'

She swung around and stalked back out of the door, her expression daring Ben to smirk at her.

Being Ben, he took the dare. 'Change your mind?' he asked her sweetly.

'Only because there's nothing to rent,' she said ungraciously.

He shrugged. 'That's the breaks.' He opened the camper door again and made a sweeping sardonic bow which made her bristle. Like a condemned prisoner climbing the gallows steps, Jessica mounted the two that led into the camper.

It was surprisingly spacious—at least that was her first impression. She revised it quickly when Ben climbed in behind her, and all at once the interior shrank remarkably.

'All the comforts of home.' Ben pointed out the small stove, the table for two, the cupboard space, the narrow bunks. Narrow bunks about two feet apart. Jess swallowed and looked away.

But then she found herself looking at Ben, and that didn't help either. For two weeks she had been trying to decide how to deal with him. At first she had been tempted to try to exact some sort of revenge, to try to pay him back for the past, for destroying her home and her family—for all the pain he had caused.

But then, partly because Gunnar was stressing responsibility, and partly because she knew that in almost every area of her life she had put her past behind her, Jessica knew she had to do the same here. So she had decided to treat Ben with indifference. She wouldn't hate him, she had told herself. He wasn't worth it. She would prove to him what a cool, competent professional she had become, and she wouldn't let on how hurt she had been all those years ago.

But in the last fifteen minutes, since she had laid eyes on him again, she knew she had her work cut out for her. It was going to be a long two weeks.

'Where do I stow my stuff, then?' she asked.

He opened one of the cupboards, kicking aside a basket of dirty laundry to do so. 'Here. And you can have this bunk.' He indicated the one next to the cupboard he offered her.

'I'm not sleeping here!'

He lifted an eyebrow.

'I'm not.'

'Got any better ideas?'

'Hundreds of them. There are motels along the way.'

'Got a reservation?'

'No.'

'It's the middle of the summer, love,' he said, as if explaining things to a slightly simple child.

'I know what time of the year it is, Mr Standish. And don't call me "love".'

'All right, Ms Mallory,' he said with exaggerated politeness. 'If you don't have a reservation, you aren't going to get a room.'

'Of course I am. It's only for one night, after all. Then we'll be at the bay.' She forebore to mention the separate tents.

'Well, if it's only for one night, why not stay here?'

'I—I—'

'You're scared.'

'Scared?' she echoed.

One dark brow lifted. 'Well, aren't you?'

'Of course not!' Jess denied vehemently. 'Why should I be?'

A corner of his mouth lifted. 'I can't imagine,' he drawled. 'Unless . . .' The smile broadened.

Jessica stared at him mutely, her heart beating like a bird trapped in her chest. 'Unless what?' she demanded at last.

'Unless the chemistry's still there.'

'What chemistry?' she croaked.

Ben clicked his tongue in mock disgust. 'Don't tell me you've forgotten?'

'On the contrary,' she snapped. 'I've got a wonderful memory. I remember very well the day I came back from letting the pelicans go. I remember my dad packing up the boat. I remember—'

'Remember this?' And before she could stop him, he bent down and caught her mouth with his, kissing her hard, branding her. The world spun crazily and Jessica moaned, trying to push him away at the same time that her traitorous body responded to him. It remembered exactly what he wanted it to remember—that elemental attraction between them, that stark, aching need that had never been quenched. She trembled, her hands gripping his shirt front as she shoved at him.

'Stop it!' she gasped, finally jerking away.

'Remember now?' His voice was soft, taunting almost, and he touched the tip of her nose for just an instant before he turned away. Then, looking over his shoulder he advised, 'Think about it,' and walked to the front of the camper with the easy nonchalance of someone who might have done no more than scratch the ears of a tabby cat.

Jessica sank against the wall oven, devastated. Her body was still screaming, *Yes*. Her mind screamed, *No*. And her emotions were in a state of shock.

'When you've stowed your gear, we can get under way,' Ben told her in a conversational tone as he slipped between the two front seats into the driver's seat. Obviously it hadn't affected him at all.

'Right.' Jessica tried to marshal her wits. She scrambled for her backpack, shoving it into the cupboard Ben had indicated and shutting the door on it, wishing she could shut the door on her feelings as well. But they were not so easily banished. And she was still trembling slightly when she wiped damp palms on the sides of her jeans and slid into the seat next to him.

'Ready now?' he asked her, his voice slightly mocking.

Was she? Jessica wondered. Or had she just jumped into a situation way over her head? She was racing to him like a juvenile, like a besotted teeny-bopper. Where was all her adult reserve? Where had all her best intentions fled to?

'As I'll ever be,' she told him with all the prim indifference she could muster, and tried to ignore the grin that lit his face.

She tried to think about White Birch Bay, tried to sort out a comprehensive plan for covering the area and tracking down any wolves that might be there in the shortest time possible. But she could not think past the man beside her. Out of the corner of her eye, she saw him back the camper out of the narrow parking space, appreciating, albeit unwillingly, the smooth control he demonstrated, the easy, man-of-the-world confidence he exuded.

That hadn't changed either. Even when the name Ben Standish was not a household word among those who appreciated fine photography and crystal-clear prose, he had had no insecurities.

She sighed and closed her eyes, remembering, not sure she wanted to, yet unable to help herself. Remembering herself at sixteen, Ben at twenty-four. She hadn't had any doubts then either. Everything was always going to work out for the best.

IT WAS GOING TO BE the best summer of her life. Sixteen-year-olds knew those sorts of things, Jess thought wryly. They were positive, confident, living in a world without doubt. And Jessica knew that that summer was going to be the turning point of her family and herself. Instead of going their separate ways, keeping in touch by the infrequent letter and even more infrequent phone call, they were all going to be together at last.

Her globe-trotting biologist father, Max, was going to spend three entire months doing an in-depth study of the flora and fauna of the Channel Islands, right off the California coastline. And her film star mother, Clarissa Evans, had signed to co-star in a movie that was going to be shot in Santa Barbara.

Jessica, who scarcely saw her parents during the school year, which she spent at St Helena's in Connecticut, could hardly wait.

'We're going to be a real family,' she told her roommate, Sarah. And Sarah, who was shunted around just as often as Jessica, was well and truly impressed.

'Maybe we'll even settle in Santa Barbara for good,' Jessica went on, dreamily embroidering her fantasies. 'Maybe they'll have another baby.'

She thought another child sounded like a wonderful idea. It would be just the thing to cement Max and Clarissa's marriage. She was longing to see a different sort of headline in the gossip mags, one that would state that *Max's Baby Proves Clarissa Has Wedded Bliss* or words to that effect. The other sort of gossip articles she had seen far too often.

She could hardly wait for the plane trip that would take her to Santa Barbara that June. And if she thought it took hours and hours, the much shorter taxi ride to the downtown beachfront hotel where they had a cottage for the summer was the longest in her life.

No one had met her at the airport, but Jessica told herself she didn't expect them to. Her parents were busy people, after all. They would welcome her at the hotel with open arms, she was sure.

Clarissa, Scotch in hand, was lounging beside the pool when Jess arrived. 'Heavens, you've grown a foot!' she exclaimed, horrified. 'Turn around.'

Jess did, dropping her suitcases and spinning round on the tile, awaiting her mother's approval.

Clarissa sighed. 'Stand up straight, do, Jessica. You've got sloping shoulders just like Max.'

Jess stood up straight.

Over the next couple of weeks she also took smaller bites, didn't laugh as loudly, and tried her best to smile without showing the braces on her teeth—all things that Clarissa demanded in no uncertain terms. But even so, Clarissa was not easily pleased.

It was easier, Jess soon discovered, to please Max.

She had inherited not only his sloping shoulders, but his interest in biology. And he never told her to stand up straighter or to talk more quietly. He simply smiled at her a vague sort of way, as if he thought she was a perfectly pleasant person, but he couldn't quite remember who she was. Except when she showed an interest in his birds or his fish. Then his eyes brightened and he looked at her with real respect. Then he willingly spent hours talking to her about his passions.

It wasn't turning into the summer Jess had been hoping for. At least not at first. But she didn't give up hope. These things took time, she reminded herself. Families didn't reunite easily overnight. So she rejoiced in the few family dinners they managed together, made herself scarce when it looked as if her parents might want to spend some time together. And she kept her fingers crossed.

Things did begin to improve. Clarissa got Max to a couple of film get-togethers. Max took Clarissa sailing. Jessica watched it all with bated breath and tiptoed to her room to fantasise the night away. She felt certain that when autumn came, Max would announce that he was going to buy a house in Santa Barbara and settle down, that Clarissa would reveal that she had taken a part in a TV series that would base her in the area, and, of course, there would be a perfectly respectable, educationally stimulating school nearby for Jess.

That, at least, was the scenario Jessica had in mind. And they would have achieved it, too, she was certain. If it hadn't been for Ben Standish.

She remembered as clearly as if it had been yesterday the moment she met him. She had eased open the door to their sumptuous hotel cottage, hoping she could sneak in and clean the afternoon's accumulation of beach sand and tar off her feet and legs before Clarissa could take her to task again, only to be confronted by both her parents and the most devastatingly attractive man she had ever seen in her life.

He was in his early twenties, with thick dark hair and a lean, rangy build accentuated by his snug denim jeans and a close-fitting ivory-coloured polo shirt. The closest Jessica, in her all-girls' school education, had come to seeing a man like this one was on the pages of Sarah's carefully preserved beefcake calendar. She could only stare.

'Honestly, look at you, Jessica!' Clarissa clinked the ice in her Scotch glass in clear disapproval.

Max's smile was more tolerant. 'This is our daughter Jessica,' he said.

The dark-haired man's eyes flicked from the beautiful Clarissa to Jessica's sandy, dishevelled body, and she detected undisguised amusement in his gold-flecked tawny eyes.

'I see,' he said, and Jess went far redder than her recently acquired sunburn when she thought about what he saw.

She knew she was no beauty. At sixteen she was long-legged, with slim hips, not much bust, and, of course, Max's sloping shoulders. 'A crane,' the boys at the military academy across the lake from St Helena's called her. And while she had her mother's colouring and bone structure, she certainly had none of Clarissa's curves or obvious beauty yet.

Nevertheless, Jessica was annoyed that she should be a source of amusement for this gorgeous man, and she met his gaze with a glare of her own.

'And who are you?' she asked ungraciously.

'Ben Standish.' He said it as if she ought to recognise it at once.

'Am I supposed to know who that is?' Jessica asked him as she wiped at the sand on her legs with a beach towel.

'Jessica!' Clarissa expostulated.

But Ben only gave a lazy, confident smile. 'You will,' he promised.

It wasn't long before she did.

Ben Standish, Jessica discovered in short order, was an up-and-coming photo-journalist who had just convinced Max Mallory to let him do an article on the Channel Islands expedition.

'It means,' he told Jessica, tweaking her long blonde braid on his way out of the suite, 'that I'll be seeing a lot more of you.'

Jessica had mixed feelings about that. The boys she had known at the military academy were one thing; Ben Standish was something else entirely.

Over the next few weeks her single-minded efforts to turn the Mallorys into a loving family unit diminished a bit. She still tried, but she didn't devote all her waking hours to it any more. Most of her waking hours, it seemed, were increasingly preoccupied with thoughts of Ben.

Her father had frequently complimented her on the thoroughness of her research and the in-depth way she studied whatever she took on. He meant the way she looked at fish and seaweed. But he could have said the same about the way she watched Ben.

Her interest, she told herself time and again, was purely academic. Just a study to discover how the human male thought and acted. Biological observation, she assured herself, then blushed wildly at the thought. She had dated, in the vague, prescribed form that all girls from St Helena's were allowed to date. But she had never entertained fantasies about Andrew Cummings at the academy that were anywhere near as vivid as those she had about Ben.

She told herself that it was because she had never seen Andrew Cummings stripped down to nothing but a pair of faded red bathing trunks while he hauled in specimen nets hand over hand in the noonday sun. She told herself it was because she had never watched Andrew sprawl comfortably on the beach and eat corn on the cob and then lick his fingers with gusto afterwards. But no matter what she told herself, she was hot and bothered every time Ben Standish was around.

He was around a lot.

Of course, he spent many hours on her father's research boat, the *Adela Star,* interviewing Max and his crew and snapping hundreds of photos. It was natural that she would see him there. She had taken to coming along on the boat before Ben even arrived. She saw no reason to stop coming just because he was there. On the contrary.

He was also around in the evenings. Max had lots of stories to tell and Ben was an appreciative audience. They would lounge by the pool, Max telling stories, Clarissa occasionally chipping in with movie tales, and Ben would listen, laugh and make notes. He would also tease Jessica. He seemed to delight in doing that. Jessica didn't know whether to be pleased with the attention or annoyed at the quality of it. She just knew that, despite her common sense, Ben Standish was fast becoming the most important person in her life.

She wasn't sure how he felt about her.

But with the confidence of the young, she made up her mind to find out. Her first chance came one evening when Clarissa had to go to Hollywood to a film premiere. She breezed into the living-room of their cottage at five that afternoon, already wearing a pink sequined evening dress, and stopped dead when she saw Max, still in his khakis and sweat-stained T-shirt, reading a close-typed monograph.

'Max—for heaven's sake! Get ready! We'll be late!'

'Late?'

Clarissa let out a squeak of rage. '*Valley Drums!* Walter Ward's new picture! For God's sake, Max, I told you yesterday.'

Max rubbed his hand across his eyes. 'Ah, Clarissa,' he began, 'I'm so bushed, I—'

'Max! You promised.'

'Jessica will go with you,' he offered. 'Won't you, Jess?'

Jessica didn't like Hollywood premieres any more than her father did, and she had no intention of offering herself as a substitute. Her parents needed time together, for heaven's sake.

'I can't, Daddy,' she lied.

Max frowned. 'Can't?'

Jessica cast around for a suitable reason not to go. The only thought in her head, as usual, was Ben. 'I'm going to the movies with Ben.'

Ben, who had been sitting at the kitchen table transcribing the notes he had made that day, looked as astonished as her parents did.

Max's eyes narrowed and he gave Ben a searching look, while Clarissa's eyes widened, then narrowed, and fixed on her daughter whose own eyes were locked with Ben's.

It seemed an eternity before he said something. Then he gave Max a slow smile. 'There's an art film out at the University tonight.'

Jessica breathed again, sending him a fleeting smile of thanks at the same moment she asked herself what she had got herself into now.

Ben asked the same question the moment Clarissa and a grumbling, reluctant Max went out of the door.

'What the hell did you say that for?'

Jessica shrugged helplessly. 'I'm sorry. I didn't want to go...I wanted them to...' She gave up, shrugging again, feeling awkward enough just being left alone with him for a change.

'Hmph,' was all she heard from Ben, and she slunk into the other room, trying to figure out what to do now.

Twenty minutes later he stood in front of her saying, 'Let's go.'

'Where?'

'To the movies, where else?'

'Oh, but we don't have to—'

'We do,' said Ben. 'I as much as told them we'd be together tonight.' He hauled her unceremoniously out of the chair.

'We can stay here!' she protested.

'No,' he said. 'We can't.'

'Why not?'

He stopped dead, his hand still wrapped around hers, jolting her with that simple contact. Their eyes met and held. 'Think about it, Jessica,' he said softly. 'I'm sure you can figure it out.'

The electricity fairly crackled between them, turning Jessica bright red. 'Oh,' she said.

'I thought you could.' Ben sounded sardonic, holding the door open for her.

They went to the movie.

CHAPTER TWO

'YOU WEREN'T the one who was supposed to come along,' Ben said abruptly, jerking Jessica out of her reverie so that she sat up straight and stared out at the forest that lined the narrow highway.

'No,' Jess conceded, relieved to forget the past for the moment.

'What happened? Did you change your plans when you found out it was me?'

'Don't flatter yourself!'

He shot her a narrow glance before turning back to the road. 'Well, when I took the assignment, they told me it was going to be with some guy called Morrow.'

'Yes—Matt. I work with him.'

'So what happened to Matt?'

'Wolves aren't really his specialty. He's a fish man mostly.'

'Then why did I get him in the first place?'

Jessica sighed, seeing that he wasn't going to let it drop until he got some sort of answer that satisfied him. 'I was going on holiday when the story first came through,' she told him.

'Oh? Where?'

'Hawaii?'

'And you dropped it all just for me?'

'My plans fell through,' Jessica replied tersely.

She had no intention of explaining to Ben exactly what had happened to them. He had no reason to know about herself and Kyle.

The trip to Hawaii hadn't ever been planned as the beginning of a tryst, even though Jessica had the feeling now that that was what Kyle had intended it to become.

In the first instance it was supposed to be simply a group of those who played volleyball together taking a summer vacation as a group. At the same time she had been seeing Kyle Walter casually. He was tall, blond and handsome, a CPA at a local firm, and more than a little charming. Jessica had thought going with a group that included Kyle might be a way to get to know him better without being expected to jump in bed with him. Kyle hadn't said he expected more than that.

Kyle, Jessica discovered, hadn't said a lot of things.

He hadn't told her, for instance, that he had a wife.

When she found that out, she was incensed. Hawaii was out of the question. Kyle was out of the question. She wanted no part of breaking up a marriage. She told Kyle to get out of her life in no uncertain terms.

But Kyle hadn't taken no for an answer.

He had appeared at her apartment, banging on the door, wheedling, 'Please, Jessie. Just listen to me. Then if you want me to go...' His voice had trailed off and Jessica, who had been peering out of the peephole, saw her landlady's curtains twitch.

Mrs Franco was a paragon of respectability. She lived a quiet life and expected the same from her tenants. Jessica was all for it. A childhood of exactly the opposite had made her that way. Reluctantly she opened the door.

Kyle followed her into the airy green and white living-room of her lakefront apartment. 'I've left Tracy for good,' he told her. 'I'm filing for divorce. We can still got to Hawaii.' He gave Jessica a hopeful, coaxing smile. But Jessica wouldn't let herself be coaxed. A married man was a married man, even if he was separated from his wife. She had no use for people who broke up other people's marriages, and she had no intention of becoming one herself. She knew how despicable that was.

'Go to Hawaii,' she said shortly, kicking off her shoes and padding across the thick forest green carpet. 'I'm not. I'm going to White Birch Bay, Michigan, to look for wolves.'

Kyle had stared at her as if she had lost her mind. He thought sand in his swimming trunks was the height of discomfort. The idea of two and a half weeks in the wilderness appalled him.

But Jessica had remained adamant. Even when she found out that she was, as Matt Morrow said, 'taking the biggest wolf with her' in the person of Ben Standish, she had made up her mind to go.

She even told herself that it would be good for her. It would help her come to terms with the past, once and for all. And perhaps, she thought, it might even help Kyle. If she weren't around, willing to be temptation, maybe he would go back to his wife. It was possible. Jessica was sure it was possible for a husband and wife to get back together again. It had to be. Even if it didn't happen in every case.

'Well,' said Ben when it was obvious she wasn't going to amplify her reasons, 'I'm glad it was you rather than Morrow. It promises to be far more interesting.' He gave her a grin that sent a shiver down her spine even though she tried to steel herself against it.

'Thank you,' she said. She tried to sound as if she thought his statement was purely professional when she knew it was anything but.

'You're welcome. Did you have a good flight?' he asked her as he pulled out to pass a car pulling a trailer.

'Yes,' said Jessica, relieved that he had decided, for the moment at least, not to pursue any worse avenues of conversation.

'I drove up,' he said. 'Spent a couple of days camping by Lake Superior.'

She didn't reply, not wanting to encourage him. The less she knew about him, the better.

'I've been living in Missouri,' he went on.

'Oh?' He had managed to pique her curiosity after all, drat him! Missouri? She had heard that he wasn't frequenting the Hollywood scene anymore. In fact, he seemed to have left the fashion and female aspects of his professional career behind in the last few years, preferring to concentrate again on the nature and wildlife photography that he had started with.

But Missouri? That seemed to be overdoing it a bit.

'Were you doing a story there?' she asked with polite indifference.

'No. I live there.'

'In this?'

'No. I've bought myself a cabin. Acres and acres of mountains and trees.'

Jessica stared. This was the man she had become accustomed to reading about in the gossip mags? The man with the splashy Beverly Hills apartment? The man with the Porsche? She expected him to grin and say, 'Just kidding,' but he didn't.

'You'd like it,' he said instead, slanting her a look that made her stiffen because it caught her off guard, shifting the focus to her again.

'How do you know?'

'I remember things, too.'

'I might have changed!'

'I don't think so.' His voice was soft, knowing. Irritating. 'Other things haven't,' he reminded her.

Jessica glared, then jerked her head away to stare out at the passing forest, knowing that the colour was high in her cheeks.

'Have they, Jess?' he prodded.

She didn't deign to answer. Her fingernails dug into the denim that hugged her thighs, and she wondered how she could ever have thought she would get through these two weeks or so with him and remain unscathed. Not even two hours had passed and already she was losing her grip on things.

It wasn't fair.

She needed to do something—anything—to prevent him infiltrating her life again. When she had first found out it would be Ben Standish with whom she would be working, she had been apprehensive, then glad.

She had told herself it would purge all the feelings she had had for him. And then she had got on with preparing for the expedition. She hadn't let herself confront those feelings. She had banished them from her mind as best she could eight years ago. It wasn't easy to face them again.

But, she decided, maybe she needed to confront them, to sort them out. Maybe she wouldn't be able to deal with him indifferently until she did so. Heaven knew she needed to do something: her reactions of the past two hours had taught her that much. She was just as vibrantly aware of him now as she had been eight years ago, God help her. It was like being sixteen all over again.

No, she thought sharply, it wasn't. She wasn't the same person she had been eight years ago. Not at all. She was grown up now. She knew better than to drool over him, follow his every move, engrave his every word on her heart.

But once she had.

Yes, God help her, once she had.

Once she had thought Ben Standish was everything she every wanted. To her sixteen-year-old mind and heart, he was everything that was good and right—strong, handsome, ambitious, talented, and loving.

Yes, she had been sure he was loving. Positive of it.

He had taken her to the movie, and he had been just as aware of her as she was of him. But he had held himself firmly under control. Only Jessica had sensed the passion he didn't release. But it was there; she felt it.

He spent a lot of time with her. He never told her to get lost. And if he had stopped teasing her after their one unorthodox movie date, choosing instead to spend the time he was with her in brooding silence, she was flattered, not chagrined. Jessica knew all about brooding silences. She understood how one could be tongue-tied and uncomfortable in the presence of the beloved. She felt much the same emotions herself.

'Eight years isn't so much,' she told him one afternoon when she was lying on a chaise-longue by the pool and Ben was pretending to read a book beside her.

'What?'

'You're only eight years older than I am,' she said. 'That's not a lot.'

'It's a lifetime, Jessica,' he growled, burying his nose in the book.

But Jessica was not deterred. 'My mother's twelve years younger than my father.'

'And look how happy they are,' said Ben, sarcasm dripping.

'They're happy!' Jess retorted. 'They're very happy!'

And if Ben looked sceptical, it was simply because he didn't know them very well. He didn't understand that Max and Clarissa weren't the garden variety of parents. But they had been married for years and years, twenty at least. So what did he know? Jessica glowered at him.

'Anyway,' she said at last, 'it's nothing to do with us.'

Ben didn't make any comment at all about that. He simply set his book down on the tile, stood up and dived straight into the pool. He was on his thirty-third lap and showed no signs of stopping when Clarissa called them for dinner.

'Were you bothering Ben again?' Clarissa asked her sharply when Jess came into the cottage.

'No.' But she crossed her fingers under the beach towel she carried. Was she bothering Ben? Heavens, she hoped so. Quite a lot.

But she didn't know for certain though until the morning of the oil spill. Instead of awakening at her regular seven a.m. alarm, Jess was jostled out of a sound sleep before it was even light. She squinted up to see Max bending over her.

'There's been a oil spill at one of the rigs near my birds. Come on.'

And Jess had stumbled out of bed, struggling into jeans, a T-shirt and a thin nylon windbreaker. Then, grabbing a bagel from the tiny cottage kitchen, she followed her father to the car park where she saw Ben, already sitting in her father's jeep.

Jess blinked, letting her still-dreamy eyes drink in the unexpected sight of him.

His dark hair was sleep-tousled and, in the blurred light of dawn, she thought his unshaven cheeks and jaw gave him a rumpled, endearing look. He wore a T-shirt identical to hers, with a stencilled tribute to Mallory's Expeditions on the front, and the same pair of faded red swimming trunks that were featured prominently in her fantasies, during most of which she was taking them off.

The colour rose swiftly in her cheeks at the thought, and grew even darker when Ben's gaze lingered on her longer than usual, too. In her hurry to join her father, she had neglected to put on a bra. She didn't have much on top to attract attention, but obviously she had enough. From where Ben's gaze remained, she knew he noticed.

'Hi.'

It was all he said, but Jessica read volumes of meaning into the word. It was a greeting, a caress, a muted longing, a need.

She shook her head, telling herself she was dreaming. But when she scrambled into the jeep next to him, she began to wonder. Her jean-clad thigh was pressed against his bare one, and he slung his arm over her shoulder, hugging her close as Max drove. It was everything she had been hoping for, and she wondered if she was going to wake up.

But as the day wore on, she knew it was no dream.

She and Ben formed a two-person team, working together along with the other volunteers. They set up the tanks that would contain liquids to help remove the oil, then together they began to scour the cliffs and beaches for the birds who had survived.

They had no time to talk, no time to stare deeply into one another's eyes. But Jessica felt the oneness that grew intangibly between them. Without so much as a word, they thought alike, moved alike. They were in tune. In love. Jessica's heart soared. She wondered what it would be like to make love with Ben. If this wordless communion would carry over to their lovemaking. If each would know instinctively what the other wanted.

She grew hot, and it wasn't just the sun.

But as morning turned to afternoon, and the sun did beat down on them, making them sweat, Jess stopped long enough to wipe her palms on her jeans and curse them. But one look at Ben's bare legs, his calves and thighs criss-crossed with abrasions and scratches that had come from wrestling with birds and scrambling over the rocks, and she didn't complain. Instead she grew concerned about him.

'You ought to put something on those cuts,' she said finally.

Ben stared down at his legs dispassionately. There was blood, dried and matted, in the dark hairs on his thighs. An open scrape oozed on his calf.

'There are more on the back,' Jess told him, trying to sound antiseptic when even looking at him made her pulses race. 'Come on. We can get you the first aid kit on the boat.'

She hadn't thought until then exactly what first aid would entail. When she did, as they were walking down the beach to the dinghy, her heart expanded in her chest, her mouth grew dry and her palms moist.

'Wait a minute,' she told him when they reached the boat. 'I'll get it.' She climbed in and rummaged through the supply box, coming up with a clean cloth, antiseptic and a bottle of fresh water.

Ben stood still, waiting.

Jessica climbed back out, then looked up at him mutely, wondering if she dared. Ben's eyes glittered with a strange fire and she licked her lips.

'Give me that.' He took the cloth from her roughly, and bent over, swabbing at the scrapes with an abrasiveness that made her wince. But at least she wasn't doing it herself. Though whether she was disappointed or not, now that the decision had been taken out of her hands, she wasn't sure.

She barely had time to wonder when he stopped and straightened up. 'You'll have to do the back,' he said.

Jess swallowed.

She took the cloth he handed her and then, biting her tongue between her teeth, she knelt in the sand and began to dab carefully at the strong well-muscled thighs just inches from her face. Her fingers grazed his skin and she sucked in her breath. She saw Ben's muscles tighten beneath her touch.

Pretend he's a pelican, she advised herself. She had spent the morning dousing them in just such a fashion with no enormous emotional investment at all.

But Ben was no pelican. And when she had at last daubed his cuts with the antiseptic and stumbled to her feet, he turned quickly and caught her, steadying her with both hands as her breasts heaved and brushed against his bare chest. Jess gulped and stared into his eyes.

The feeling that had been smouldering between them since the day they had met leapt to life in that instant. Now there was no pool to dive into, no movie to watch, no Max or Clarissa watching to put a damper on things.

'Ah, Jess,' Ben whispered, agonized. It was a groan both of dismay and surrender, and it only ceased when his lips touched hers.

There had never been a kiss like that one in the history of the universe. It was warm, sweet, needing, demanding. And like a thirsty desert flower in a springtime rain, Jessica opened to it, responding, blossoming under its touch. Her soft lips gave to his, savouring his taste, delighting in the warm, slightly salty taste of his mouth. She sighed, blessed with the certain knowledge that, however wonderful her fantasies had been, reality was miles better.

'Jessica!' Max's voice rang out in the distance, but she scarcely heard.

It was Ben who stumbled back, shaken, his breath coming raggedly, his eyes glazed. 'Oh, God,' he muttered. 'I want—'

Jessica leaned towards him to kiss him again, to soothe away the anguish she saw in his face, to give him what she knew quite clearly that he wanted. But he shook his head vehemently, and he thrust her away.

'Don't, Jess! No! For God's sake!' His eyes skittered away from her. 'Go see what your dad wants.'

'But, Ben—'

'Go on!' He practically shoved her towards the cliff where Max and the crew were working. 'Go on!

Get!' And he turned and strode quickly down the beach in the opposite direction.

Confused, Jess looked after him, then went off to seek Max. It was as if, for one shining moment, the whole world was perfect, and then had slipped out of kilter again. Ben's kiss made perfect sense to her. His reaction afterwards didn't at all. Unless he was worried about what Max would think. Yes, that must be it. Perhaps he thought her father would disapprove.

'Help me with these baby pelicans,' Max told her, hardly turning around.

Jessica helped, her mind still kissing Ben, thinking that he needn't have worried. Max wouldn't have noticed them at all unless they sprouted wings and flew.

She spent the rest of the afternoon helping her father. She kept expecting Ben to come and pair up with her again. But he didn't. In fact, he seemed intent on staying as far away as he could. She wanted to tell him it was all right. But he was involved with helping Shorty Lyle, her father's captain, and the only time she got near him, all she managed to say was, 'What about us?'

Ben coloured faintly, but he didn't smile. He just looked grim and said quite sharply, 'I'm just doing what's needed most, Jessica. You should too.' And he shouldered a basket of birds Shorty passed him and moved away.

'Jess,' said Max, his tone impatient, and she had no choice but to go and help her father again.

They kept busy until almost dusk. Finally, muscles aching, mind spinning, Jess was only too glad to sink down on the deck of the *Adela Star* as it churned through choppy seas back to the harbour. She leaned against the wheelhouse, cradling in her lap two baby pelicans wrapped in a towel. Their mother had died. They were close to gone, too. Only pure stubbornness wouldn't allow her to give up on them. They needed her, and it seemed at the moment that they might be the only ones who did.

Her eyes sought Ben. He was standing at the far end of the deck, his forearms resting on the rail as he stared out at the horizon. She willed him to turn and look at her, to come and sit beside her, to share again the feelings and the closeness that they had experienced earlier today.

He did turn. He did look at her, his eyes squinting hard into the sun. They met hers for a long moment, then wavered, dropped. And he turned away.

Jess sighed, tasting defeat, not understanding what had happened. One of the pelicans poked her hand and she stroked it absently, but her mind was still mulling over Ben. Was this love? Or what? And would she ever figure him out?

She was no nearer having done so when the *Adela Star* reached the still waters of the harbour, nudging

the tyre-rimmed slip where it was berthed. The first
sound Jess heard was the voice of her mother.

'For God's sake, Max,' she shrilled. 'It's past
eight-thirty! We're supposed to be at Victor's right
now!'

'It's only a party, Clarissa!'

'It's my career, damn you!'

Jess raised herself slightly to peer over the side.
Clarissa was standing on the dock, her hands on hot
pink, silk-clad hips, her evening gown a direct coun-
terpoint to the grubby utilitarian *Adela Star* and her
equally grubby, oil-spattered, fishy-smelling owner.

'And this is *my* career, Clarissa,' Max retorted. He
shoved an angry hand through his hair and glared
down at his wife.

Please, Daddy, just go with her, Jess prayed. Be
pleasant. Don't fight. Don't let there be any more
hurt and confusion tonight. Her own was enough.

'They're only birds, Max,' pouted Clarissa.
'Dumb, stupid birds!'

Max muttered something unintelligible then, and
when Clarissa didn't let up, shouted down to her, 'Go
by yourself, then! Or take Standish! This is important, Clarissa! This is work!'

There was a stunned silence. Jessica held her
breath, waiting for her mother's tirade, for the tears
that threatened. They never came.

Instead she heard Clarissa say in a cool, almost detached voice, 'What a marvellous idea. You'd enjoy a cast party, wouldn't you, Ben?'

Please, no! Jess thought, stabbed, her world splintering when she heard Ben reply, 'I think I might.'

He couldn't mean it. She stared at him, aghast. But he gave her a hard look, as if daring her to contradict him. Then he strode past her, and she heard a warm, almost eager note in his voice as he vaulted over the side of the boat and said to her mother, 'Sounds great, Clarissa. Don't mind if I do!'

It was an indication of how basically naive, foolish and totally besotted she was, Jessica thought now as she stared out the camper window, that she had managed to rationalise even that.

She had gone back to the cottage, nursing her misery, wondering at the agony of true love, hating her mother and Ben and, at the same time, trying her best to understand why he had gone off like that.

It didn't even take her very long. He was keeping the peace, she decided. He was trying to smooth things over between Max and Clarissa, trying to help Jessica in her quest for the ideal family.

She tasted bitter bile even now remembering what she had managed to believe. Oh, fool, she chided herself. Oh, lovesick, foolish, foolish girl.

But she had told herself that he couldn't kiss her the way he had that afternoon, couldn't feel that much passion for her, and then turn to her mother for company. Not for *that* kind of company at any rate.

But turn to Clarissa he did.

In fact, after that night when she took him to the cast party as a substitute for Max, she seemed to be dragging him everywhere. To be sure, he still hung around Max and the *Adela Star* often enough. But he seemed to be scrupulously avoiding Jess. It hurt, it made her angry. It made her jealous even, though she told herself that was insane. Clarissa was fifteen years older than Ben, for heaven's sake!

But it didn't seem to matter to Clarissa. She found him plenty of jobs taking pictures of her rich and beautiful friends. She introduced him to film stars and starlets, encouraging him to take photos of them. And it was obvious that he liked that. Jess knew he was ambitious. She had known it from the moment they had met. But she hadn't thought it would take him away from her, and she wanted to ask him whether taking pictures of lovely ladies and handsome gents was as fulfilling as the time he spent on the *Adela Star*—as the time he had spent with her. But she hardly saw him to be able to ask.

She busied herself with her pelicans, taking heart from the fact that they seemed to be gaining strength each day. And she allowed herself to take heart, too, from the fact that there seemed to be no more obvious outbursts between Max and Clarissa. Her father was pursuing his work with the single-minded intensity to which she had grown accustomed, and Clarissa, having Ben as an escort, seemed satisfied with that.

It wasn't ideal, and Jessica knew it. But considering the alternatives, perhaps it was the best that could be hoped.

Sometimes she still fancied that Ben was spending time with Clarissa just because he knew how much Jess wanted things calm and smooth. She often caught him watching her from a distance, even when he was supposedly dancing attendance on Clarissa at some function or other. And now and then she thought she detected both hunger and sympathy in his eyes.

Clarissa seemed to see it, too, for she frequently became shrill in her demands just then, and Ben would recollect himself and jump to do her bidding. But later Jess would look up and find his eyes following her again.

She wanted to ask him what he truly felt. But she never saw him alone. She was either busy helping Max—and he was demanding more and more of her time as he discovered how competent she was—or Clarissa had Ben with her. There was a tension in the air, she could feel it. But it was like nothing she had felt before or could put a name to. Still, she wanted desperately to understand.

The summer was coming to a close. Ben was writing the last part of his article and would be moving on soon. Max was finishing his study. The movie was almost under wraps. Even the birds were well enough to let go. It was a time of change. School was going to start in two weeks. Jess had one more year, then college. But she couldn't go back without talking to Ben, without getting a sense of how he was feeling, without at least asking if he would wait for her.

'I'm going to let the birds go tomorrow,' she said casually one afternoon when she came out to find her mother and Ben beside the pool.

Clarissa didn't even look up. 'It's about time.'

Jess swallowed, then forced herself to say the words she had been saying over and over in her head since yesterday morning when she had decided. 'Do you want to come?' she asked Ben.

She half—no, more than half—expected him to say no. He had been avoiding her for so long.

But he sat up straighter, suddenly more alert. 'Tomorrow?' He shot a quick glance at Clarissa, who raised an eyebrow at him. He cleared his throat, 'When?'

'After lunch?' said Jess, hopes rising. 'Say about one?'

He still seemed to be considering. 'Where?'

'I thought I'd take them back to the point where we found them.'

'Ah.' Ben trailed his fingers in the water, staring down at the ripples that fanned out from them. 'Tell you what,' he said at last, looking up at her. 'I've got a few things to do here and I don't know quite when I'll finish. You go on without me. Take the dinghy, why don't you? And I'll drive down the coast to meet you when I get away. OK?'

Jess felt the smile all over her face. 'OK.'

Ben didn't smile at all. 'You'll wait?'

For ever, Jess wanted to say. 'I'll wait.'

Ben let out a long pent-up breath. 'Good.'

JESS HAD waited. All afternoon. Then, as the sun began to disappear, so did her hopes. And as nightfall came, so did despair. He wasn't coming. Had he ever meant to come?

Numbly she opened the crate in which she had carried the pelicans, lifting them carefully out on to the sand. They waddled around uncertainly, assessing her with dark beady eyes. She tossed them each a fish.

'Have a good life,' she told them solemnly. And without letting herself think about her own life, she clambered back in the dinghy and headed home.

She putted into the harbour to discover Max stowing a pile of duffle bags on the *Adela Star*. He was working smoothly, evenly, methodically, like a well-oiled, precision machine. Jess frowned.

'What's up?' she asked.

'We're moving on to the boat.'

'But—'

'I've packed all your gear.'

'But—'

'We're leaving tonight.'

'But I have to see Ben!'

Max stopped flat on the deck and fixed her with a level stare. 'He's gone,' he told her without flinching. 'He took off this afternoon with your mother.'

CHAPTER THREE

AND THAT WAS THAT, Jessica thought as she glanced sideways at the man who had turned her life upside down all those years ago.

In short order Max and Clarissa were divorced, Jessica was shunted back to school in Connecticut, Clarissa had nailed down a juicy part in a new picture, and Max was off in the *Adela Star* to do something with sharks off the Great Barrier Reef of Australia.

And it was all Ben Standish's fault.

Suddenly she had to ask him the question that had been plaguing her all these years, the one that had nagged her night after night. It wasn't fair to her not to ask him. She needed to know.

'Why did you leave with my mother, Ben?' she asked him, point blank.

For a second he seemed taken aback, as if he hadn't expected that she would dare ask. Then he rubbed his fingers around the back of his neck, to ease the tension, she supposed, and to give himself time to come up with a plausible lie.

There weren't any, she wanted to tell him. She had tried telling herself a million, but she had never been convinced by a one of them. But never in all those years had she tried to believe what he told her then.

'Because she asked me to,' he said.

'What?'

He stared back at her, unblinking. 'Because she asked me to,' he repeated.

'I don't believe that!' Clarissa might have been weak, she might have even been tempted to stray, but Jessica could not believe that her mother had been the one to ask! Not Clarissa Evans! Not ever!

Jess's fingers were clenched, her nails digging painfully into the palms of her hands.

'It's the truth,' Ben told her steadily, not taking his eyes from the road.

'I don't believe you,' Jessica maintained.

'You don't know what went on between your parents, Jess,' he said, his voice patient, as if she were a slightly dim child.

'And you did?' she countered angrily.

'A bit. More than you, that's for sure.'

'I knew my parents very well. Especially my father!'

'Crushed, was he, when Clarissa left?' asked Ben, his tone sardonic.

'Of course he was!'

Ben glanced at her, his doubt apparent.

'He was!' Jessica practically shouted at him. 'My father was a quiet man, for heaven's sake. He wasn't some Mafia type who was going to take a contract out on you. And he didn't spill his guts to the press. But that doesn't mean it didn't hurt him!'

'I see,' said Ben, but he didn't sound convinced.

Jessica wished she could come up with some incontrovertible evidence that would prove to Ben how much his actions had hurt her father. But the truth was, Max hadn't seemed outraged.

He was angry, of course, the day that it happened. But within a few more days, he appeared resigned. In fact, Clarissa's desertion hardly seemed to affect him at all. Jessica supposed it was because he was more or less used to getting along without her. After all, Clarissa wasn't ever around a lot. But Max had set about his work at once, and had quickly become more preoccupied than ever. It was his way, Jessica decided, of handling the pain.

He seemed to count on her more, too. He had learned that summer just how interested she was in pursuing a career in biology and also how good she was at her work. He was delighted. In fact, most of the comments he made thereafter concerning Clarissa were oblique ones—ones that said more about how glad he was to have Jessica at least, Jessica whom he could trust.

Jess remembered how glad she had been that she had been able to help, to make up in some way for her mother's vanishing. Hurt herself by Ben's desertion and betrayal, she had thrown herself into helping her father. It was a way of persuading herself that she was really her father's daughter after all. It was also a way of making up for the guilty feelings she had about allowing herself to be taken in by the suave Standish charm in the first place.

So she threw herself into helping Max for the rest of the summer, and when she went back to St Helena's in the fall, she thought she was getting over her pain. It couldn't last for ever, she told herself. She had experienced the worst of it. There was no way Ben could hurt her more.

She was wrong. Several months later he did.

It was December, nearly the end of term, and Jessica was studying hard, not letting herself remember anything beyond her assignments and the papers she had to write. She was sitting on her bed, reading, with the door opened and Sarah of the beefcake calendar came into her room. She looked at Jessica with an expression rife with pity, interest and suppressed excitement.

'You should see what Maxwell gave me,' she said, concealing something under her duffle coat.

Jess looked up from her bed, thinking that whatever it was, it had to be better than reading *Silas*

Marner which was what she was supposed to be doing. So she sat up, intrigued, and said, 'Show me.'

Sarah seemed to hesitate. Then she said, plumping herself down on the bed next to Jess, 'Well, you might not be pleased. In fact, I'm sure you won't. But we thought you ought to know, Maxwell and I.'

'What is it?' Jess frowned.

Sarah pulled a magazine out from beneath her coat, handing it to Jess. It was one of the sort that Maxwell so often showed up with, one with a fairly wild reputation. And Jessica wondered for about two seconds just what it was she was not supposed to like.

Then she saw. CLARISSA EVANS—it proclaimed in bright blue capitals—THE WOMAN ONLY HER LOVER KNOWS.

'Oh God,' she mumbled, and with trembling fingers, opened the magazine.

'Page 26,' Sarah offered helpfully.

Jessica looked, but only for a moment. She saw all she needed to see in one quick glimpse.

Yes, there was her mother, intimate, teasing, sexy—wearing just enough to preserve her modesty, yet little enough to titillate even the dullest imagination. It was Clarissa, all right, and yet it didn't seem like the woman Jess knew as her mother at all.

She slammed the magazine shut, sucking in her breath sharply.

'Her lover?' Sarah said hesitantly. 'Did they mean the fellow she...she, er, left...left your father... for? That photographer fellow?'

Jessica shuddered as the awful possibility grew in her mind.

That photographer fellow ... photographer ... 'The woman only her lover knows' ... photographer ...

Oh God, Ben, how could you?

She ripped open the magazine again, scanning the pages of the article, searching for a photo credit, but there was none. She looked through the table of contents frantically, praying that she would find someone else's name. She didn't.

There was nothing linking it to Ben, of course.

Nothing but her own mind. Nothing but his occupation, the circumstances of her mother's departure, the way the gossip magazines linked them all the time.

Oh God, Ben!

Jessica felt sick.

She felt even sicker a month later when the gossip magazines rumoured that Clarissa Evans and Ben Standish were no longer an item. Clarissa, it seemed, had left him for a slick-smiling Hollywood star. She ought to have been glad, Jessica told herself. It would serve him right to be on the receiving end of a little rejection.

But in her own mind she felt it just confirmed her fears about the pictures. Ben must have taken them and, discovering his betrayal, Clarissa must have ended their relationship.

It had to have been that way. Otherwise Ben would have denied taking them, and he never did. He never did!

Jessica could still feel sick about those photos just thinking about them. Even now, remembering the night she had seen them, she grew cold and her throat felt as though there was a football where her larynx ought to be.

She wondered what Ben would say if she asked him about them.

She certainly wasn't the only one who had come to that conclusion. Rumours had been rampant, but neither he nor Clarissa ever spoke about them to anyone as far as Jess knew.

Jess wondered if Ben would claim that Clarissa had asked him to take them the same way he had claimed she asked him to go away with her. Probably, she thought. He seemed to have his own version of the truth.

But she wasn't going to ask. She had had quite enough lies and gibberish from him for one day. They had two and a half weeks ahead of them that they would have to spend exclusively in one another's company. Two and a half weeks, for heaven's sake!

If they were going to get through it without killing each other, there were obviously going to have to be some topics that would be off-limits for the duration. The suggestive photos of Clarissa was one of them.

But even as she made up her mind not to speak to Ben about them, Jessica still didn't censor the glower she gave him. And as if he sensed her disapproval, Ben took his eyes from the road long enough to seek hers.

'I'm sorry if you were hurt, Jess,' he said quietly.

'You're sorry?' Jessica almost snorted in combined distrust and disbelief. What a paltry few words he seemed to think would make up for having ripped her family asunder and betrayed her trust and that of her father!

'I am,' he insisted, his voice still soft. 'I didn't want to hurt you.'

'Kind of you,' Jess snarled. She jerked her gaze away to stare out of the window, refusing even to entertain the notion that he might mean what he said.

He seemed about to say something more, but Jessica's closed expression must have deterred him. Shrugging slightly, he turned his attention back to his driving, leaving her with all sorts of questions in her head that she wasn't sure if she wanted answers for or not.

The miles sped by unheeded. Not until Ben shifted in his seat and said, 'I'm getting hungry,' did Jessica realise that it was well past supper time.

'We can stop in the next town,' she suggested, realising for the first time that she was beginning to feel a bit hungry herself.

'Not much between here and where we're stopping,' said Ben. 'I've got plenty of food in the camper. Why don't you fix something while I drive?'

Jess would have preferred a restaurant. She didn't like this close confinement with Ben Standish; a little public relief wouldn't have been amiss. But she didn't want to say so. She wanted to retain her impression of indifference at all costs. And she knew he would pounce immediately on her refusal to eat in the camper with him. He would think she was afraid.

She was. But she agreed, anyway.

She slid out of the captain's chair passenger seat and made her way carefully back to the kitchen area, ferreting through the refrigerator and setting out what she found on the small table. She made ground beef into patties, then laid out buns and condiments. Opening a can of fruit, she slopped some into bowls, added cottage cheese, then laid pickles and chips on plates. As she worked she found herself grateful for the activity. It stopped her remembering, and that was good.

Finally she called out, 'Everything's ready but the cooking. Can you stop somewhere for that?'

'Sure.'

Ben found a roadside rest stop a few miles further on and pulled in, parking the camper under towering pine trees. Switching off the ignition, he swung out of the driver's seat and stretched tall, suddenly looming large in the confines of the camper and making Jessica very nervous indeed.

'Why don't you just go stretch your legs or something,' she suggested. 'I'll cook the hamburgers.'

'I can help,' he offered.

'No.'

'You sure?'

Never more sure of anything in her life. 'Just go,' Jessica said, opening the door for him. 'I'll call you when they're ready.'

She cooked them on a very low flame, wanting as much time as she could get since she wasn't getting any space. But even the time wasn't enough. And Ben was back before she called him.

While he had been out of sight, she had told herself she could handle the way he made her feel. But the moment he strode up the steps and entered the camper again, she knew she was wrong.

She tried to hide it, sitting down and putting together her sandwich, ignoring the man who sat across from her.

But he wasn't easy to ignore. Especially not when he leaned forward, resting both his elbows on the table and asked her, 'How long have you been working for NRRI?'

'A little over a year,' she told him around a mouthful of burger.

'Why aren't you working with Max?'

'He died,' she said baldly, surprised that he didn't know.

Ben frowned. 'I'm sorry.'

Jessica bit back the 'I'll bet' that threatened to fall from her lips. Pressing her mouth into a line, she nodded.

'He was a good biologist,' Ben said. 'A good man,' he added, almost as an afterthought.

'Yes,' Jess agreed. Her father had taught her a lot, had demanded a lot. He had been an inspiration of sorts, his dedication to his work amazing her, and giving her a lot to live up to. 'A damned sight better man than you,' she added, because suddenly she couldn't help herself.

Ben's brows drew together suddenly and he glared at her. The silence between them carried an almost electrical charge.

She waited for him to speak, for him to attack her right back. But he didn't say anything until he had completely finished his bun and wiped his mouth on a paper napkin.

Then he stood up slowly and deliberately, put his palms flat on the table and stared down at her. 'If you're as biased about your work as you are about your memories,' he told her quietly, 'I'm going to be able to write one hell of a story.'

Jessica's eyes widened. She sprang to her feet, nearly tipping the table between them. 'Biased? How dare you call my memories biased?'

'You doubt every word I say. It's obvious.'

'I don't need your words,' she told him sourly. 'I was there myself, remember?'

'I remember very well.'

'Then don't try to tell me how it was. I know!'

'Jess,' he began, but she cut him off.

'Just leave things alone, Ben. *Leave them alone!* It's over. We're professionals meeting on a professional basis for the sake of this study. And that's all we are.'

'And we're going to behave in a totally professional, unbiased impartial manner?' Ben mocked her, leaning back against the cupboard and regarding her with an amusement that infuriated her.

'Yes,' she snarled, 'that's exactly what we're going to do.'

She picked up her paper plate and crumpled it in her hand, then turned smartly and flung it into the waste bag.

'Whatever you say, Jessica,' he told her easily, and pushed himself away from the wall. 'But, Jess,' he added when she started to turn away from him. He reached out and touched her gently on the line of her jaw. 'I don't think that in all respects, you're as impartial as you'd like.'

CHAPTER FOUR

HEAVEN HELP HER, how true that was!

Jessica ran her fingers along her tingling jawbone as she stared at the back of Ben's head while he started up the camper. But she was damned well going to work on it. Starting now.

'I'm going to stay back here,' she told him, clearing off the table and putting the supper things away. 'I need to make some notes.'

What she needed to do, she thought wryly as she sat down at the table and forced herself to concentrate on some material Gunnar had given her right before she left, was to write five hundred times, *I will ignore Ben Standish.*

She forced herself to focus on the material from Gunnar, refusing to glance up no matter how far she thought they had travelled, until suddenly Ben called out, 'Hang on!' and she found herself having to do just that as all at once the camper bounced off the main highway and began jolting down what felt like a very rocky gravel road.

'What's this?' she asked, standing up and going to join him at the front, scowling out the window as she did so. It was nearly dusk now and a niggling awareness that she had been duped was beginning to get through to her.

'Campground,' Ben said succinctly.

'What about my motel?'

'What motel?'

'I'm not staying in here with you!'

He shrugged but didn't slow down. 'Just as soon as I stop, you can walk back.'

'Ben!'

He shot her a quick grin. 'Can't be more than eight or ten miles to the nearest town,' he told her. 'And chances are they won't have a motel even if you do get there. Probably not more than three hundred people in the whole town.'

'Then take me back to Escanaba!'

'No way.' And the camper continued its jerky trail through the dense forest, as impervious to Jessica's fury as Ben obviously was.

'Ben!' she tried again.

'Where's your impartiality now?' he taunted.

Her teeth snapped together.

'Keep an eye out for site number fourteen,' he instructed her. 'That's ours.'

But Jessica did nothing of the sort. She stood fuming, braced between the table and his chair, debating the best way to deal with him, unsure what she ought to do next.

'Ah, there it is.' He slowed down and eased the camper into the narrow clearing between the pine trees, then cut the engine and leaned back against the seat, closing his eyes. When he opened them a moment later, he fixed her with a tired grin.

'It's not much different from a motel anyway, Jess. Take a look.' He waved a hand in a sort of all-encompassing gesture.

He was right. It wasn't. There were campers and tents every fifteen or twenty feet. As soon as he shut off the engine she could hear the sound of jam boxes, children howling, dogs barking. She could smell food cooking, the scents of grease, wood smoke and mosquito repellent filling the air.

'Is this what they're planning for White Birch Bay?' Ben asked her, his tone baiting.

Jessica frowned. 'You know better than that. They only want minimal development. Nothing like this.'

'Yes.' His voice had an ominous ring.

'Never,' she replied, hoping it was true. *She* certainly didn't want it to turn out like this. And if there were wolves there, it wouldn't. They probably wouldn't want to battle conservationists and environmentalists enough even to try. At least that was her notion of what would happen.

'We'll see.' Ben got up and moved past her into the living area. He opened the refrigerator and pulled out a can of beer, popped the top off and swallowed a long draught. 'Want one?' he asked, changing the subject entirely.

'No, thank you.' The room seemed to be shrinking again. It did every time he got out of the driver's seat. Hesitating only a split second, she turned and opened the storage cabinet and hauled out her backpack. Then she headed for the door.

Ben straightened up abruptly. 'Here, where do you think you're going?'

Jess opened the door, and hopped down the two steps on to the earth. 'Out. I'm pitching my tent.'

He bounded out after her, frowning. 'Don't be an idiot!'

'There's nothing idiotic about it.' She crossed the clearing and chose a spot beneath a towering fir tree, dropped her backpack, and knelt to rummage around inside it for her small nylon tent. The idiotic thing would be to remain inside the camper with Ben; she knew that at once. Her feelings about him were all in a muddle, and she knew she couldn't be accountable for a thing she did or said until she had got control of herself and her feelings again.

'For God's sake,' he muttered, but he didn't try to stop her.

He apparently had glanced around enough to notice that several people from other sites seemed interested in the newcomers. Jess was relieved that he didn't want to give them a real show. She had learned to hate the limelight as a child. She would go to considerable lengths to avoid it now. She might have even acquiesced and returned to the camper if he had pushed it. She was glad he hadn't.

She was, however, terribly aware of his silent, scowling disapproval as she spread out her tent and staked it down, then ran the poles through the loops and erected it.

Every time she turned toward the camper she could see his dusty hiking boots planted in the dirt and the slight spread of his stance which seemed to draw her eyes inexorably upward along the inverted V of his legs. She ducked her head and resisted the temptation to look.

Finishing with the tent, she crawled inside it and unrolled her sleeping bag, glad to be out of his sight for a moment. Though as she expected when she emerged a few moments later, Ben hadn't moved away.

'I wonder,' she said sweetly, 'if I might use a bit of your running water. I'd like to brush my teeth.'

'Be my guest,' he growled, and Jess knew a moment's pleasure that she had annoyed him this time.

It might be the only time, she reminded herself as she brushed her teeth and regarded her solemn features in the tiny mirror. So enjoy it.

'Goodnight, Ben,' she said, passing him again and ducking down to crawl into her tent. She zipped it from the inside, then lifted the opaque flap for just a minute to peer through the screen. 'Pleasant dreams.'

'You, too,' he said roughly as he wheeled around and strode towards the camper. She heard what sounded like a boot colliding with a rock that skittered across the ground and clanked against the hubcap of the truck. From his tone she didn't think he was planning on anything very pleasant at all.

The first round, she decided, was a draw. Advantage, Standish.

She had to be honest and admit that, at least. She lay back on top of her bedroll and stared at the dark nylon only three feet above her face, and wondered how she was going to manage to stay even, let alone come out ahead in this little journey they were making together.

Obviously she had made a tactical error by thinking that he wouldn't have bothered to do some checking about how his companion, J.D. Mallory, was. And she seemed to have made even a bigger error in believing that he might possibly felt a bit of shame or remorse for his profligate behaviour with her mother. Clearly he didn't know the meaning of either word. And she was beginning to doubt, frankly, if she could be the one to teach them to him. Her own emotions were too fuzzy. Her clear-cut animosity and anger blurred the moment she was within five yards of him. She couldn't think straight when he was around.

The best thing to do then was keep him at a distance. Maybe when she had time to be around him some more this crazy attraction she still felt would wear off. Maybe it was simply a remnant from her childhood, something she needed to try on just to prove to herself that it didn't fit. Because, God knew, she didn't want it to fit! She loathed what he had done. She couldn't imagine getting involved with him again. Heavens, she hadn't even wanted anything to do with Kyle, and in her book Ben Standish was twenty times worse!

'Just keep away from me, Ben Standish,' she growled into her jacket which she had bunched up as a pillow. 'And I'll do my damnedest to keep away from you!'

IN THE MIDDLE of the night a storm broke, sudden and furious. Jess burrowed deeper into her sleeping bag, listening to the wind soughing through the trees, feeling it buffet her thin nylon shelter. Rain whipped against the side of the tent, and jagged bursts of lightning lit up its narrow confines for brief moments, then she was plunged into darkness again.

'Oh, for a motel,' she muttered. But she really didn't mind a lot. She had survived plenty of them before, and she would again. Besides, it was better than the camper. And that had been her only other alternative.

Another sharp burst of lightning jagged through the sky, almost blinding her with its intensity. And, oddly, the light seemed to stay on, diffusing the whole area outside her tent.

Jess wriggled half-way out of her sleeping bag and edged up the flap to glance around. Ah, there was a light on in Ben's camper.

She dropped the flap and lay back down again, relieved that so far she was staying dry. The last thing she wanted to do tonight was find herself forced to crawl out of the tent and bang on Ben's door looking for shelter.

She didn't need any 'I told you so's,' spoken or unspoken, not after she had made such a production about making her own accommodation.

She smiled and blessed her father for making her so comfortable in storms. It was one of his few real contributions to her life, sitting with her in the darkness, holding her on his lap as they watched the lightning flash and tremble in the sky and felt the thunder shake the earth beneath their feet.

'Isn't it beautiful?' Max would ask her softly, reserving for nature some of his greatest pleasure and awe.

'Yes,' Jessica would agree. It was.

She sent a silent prayer of thanks now for her father having given her that.

The ground shook again. More lightning, green and white, split the sky. The rain suddenly gave way to hail, then turned as quickly back to rain again. But the hail had done its damage. Several small leaks were beginning to drip into the tent. Most of them were on one side, the windward side, and Jess rolled her sleeping bag over to the other.

All at once she heard a sharp bang, more metallic than most of the banging of the thunder. And she heard Ben's voice, loud and harsh directly outside her tent.

'Jess, come on! Get out of there!'

She lifted up on one elbow. 'I'm fine. Go back inside.'

'You'll get drenched out here!'

'I'm not a bit wet!'

'Jess, for God's sake, get out of that tent and come in the camper!'

The hail started again and the lightning flickered. She heard Ben swear.

'Don't worry about me!' she called out to him. He was getting far wetter out there than she was in the tent.

At that second there was another terrific burst of lightning and an earth-shaking crash of thunder. The zipper of the front of her tent was ripped up, and strong hands reached in to yank her out.

'Ben Standish! Ben! Let me go!'

'No!'

And the next thing Jess knew, he had her, sleeping bag and all, flung over his shoulder and was carrying her back to the camper. She kicked him, flailed her arms, beating him on the back while he jerked open the door, then dumped her unceremoniously on the carpeted floor. Stumbling in after her, he yanked the door shut behind them.

Jessica glared at him, her breath coming in short, angry gasps.

Nostrils flared, eyes glinting, completely drenched, Ben stared back.

Then lightning flashed, thunder roared, and involuntarily he winced.

'You could have got killed out there,' he said roughly. 'A friend of mine once did. You think it can't happen to you, but it can, believe me! And even if you don't get struck by lightning, you're still soaking wet!'

'Thanks to you I'm soaking wet,' she retorted, shaking water out of her hair. 'I was perfectly all right where I was.'

'You'll be better in here.'

'All my gear is getting drenched out there.'

'It'll be all right,' he said, dismissing it.

'Like hell it will.' She scrambled to her feet, furious. 'You want me in here so bad, all right. But you can damned well go back out and get my pack!'

Ben shook his head. 'In the morning.'

'Ben,' Jess began, her voice low and ominous.

But Ben was immovable. 'Not in the storm. Morning's soon enough.' And he began stripping off his wet shirt. Jessica, without wanting to, watched as the body she remembered so well came into view again.

The hair on his chest seemed darker and thicker than she remembered it. It was sprinkled liberally across his well-developed pectorals, then tapered slightly as it arrowed downward, becoming a narrow trail where it disappeared into his jeans. Jessica swallowed hard and looked away.

'Well, if you won't get it, I will,' she said abruptly, and headed for the door.

But before she could reach it, Ben grabbed her, both hands wrapping her upper arms in a vice-like grip. 'Not now.' His voice was sharp, intense, and punctuated by another loud crash-bang of thunder.

'Jeez,' he muttered, and his fingers dug into her arms, almost bruising them.

'Ow! Ben, you're hurting me!' She looked at him closely. His eyes were dilated even in the bright inside light, and she could almost sense the throb of his heartbeat even through the grip of his hands on her arms.

'Sorry.' He dropped his hands, clenching them into fists, then jamming them into the pockets of his wet jeans. 'Just—just don't go out there, Jess. Just don't.' This time it soundly oddly like a plea, not a command. And, with it put that way, Jessica was more willing to consider it.

'Everything will get soaked,' she argued, but more mildly this time.

'Everything will dry.' He dismissed her gear easily. 'You're safe in here, though.'

'I was safe enough out there.'

'Mmm.' His only response was close to a grunt. His wolf's eyes bored into her, though, and she didn't really feel like fighting with him any more. She was tired. Obviously he was. Both of them needed their sleep.

'All right.' She kicked off her wet socks and stepped over her sopping wet bedroll, giving it a wry grimace as she did so.

'What am I supposed to sleep in?' she asked him. The thunder was receding, the lightning flickers less intense. But she doubted somehow that he would willingly let her back out to her tent.

He grinned slightly, apparently relieved that she had stopped fighting. 'My arms?' he offered, lifting a brow.

'Funny,' said Jessica, feeling a flicker of irritation. She eyed the door, and he got the hint.

'I have an old army blanket,' he offered gruffly before she could move toward the exit.

'Swell,' said Jess. 'You use it then. It's only fair since you got mine wet.'

Ben scowled. Then, as if thinking better of it, he shrugged. 'All right.'

'And a shirt?' she asked him. 'I'll need to borrow a shirt.'

'Sure.' He ferreted one out of the cupboard and handed it to her, looking far happier about that than he did about the scratchy dark green army blanket he unearthed at the same time.

'Thank you,' said Jessica with what she hoped was cool indifference. She carried the shirt into the tiny lavatory at the end of the camper.

It gave her an odd sensation to be putting on Ben's shirt, as if her very nerve ends were standing at attention. She fumbled with buttoning it, and told herself it was because she was tired and wet and cold. Not because it was Ben's shirt.

Though lean, Ben was still bigger than she was, and the shoulders hung well off hers and the shirt tails hit her mid-thigh. Good, she thought, for her jeans were damp and clammy, and she had no desire to spend the rest of the night wearing them.

She shrugged them off and rolled them up. Then, telling herself that everything would be fine, she went back out to where Ben was.

He had put on a pair of dry jeans in her absence. But his chest was still bare, and she felt entirely too aware of him. She wondered if he knew how seductive he looked, sprawled on the narrow bench beside the tiny table. Probably he did. Ben was a past master at seduction, as she well knew.

Their eyes met. Then his travelled leisurely down the length of her body, and Jessica felt as if they stripped the shirt off her as they went. She should have left her jeans on, she thought. Ben's gaze would have dried them in no time at all. Her teeth snapped together irritably, but she schooled herself to remain still under his eyes.

Let him look, she thought. Let him see what he's not going to get. He might have had my mother, but, by God, he won't have me!

Ben's fingers clenched against his thighs. 'God, you're beautiful,' he breathed.

Eight years ago Jessica would have killed to hear those words. Now she turned away, heart slamming against her chest, totally ignoring him. She laid her clothes with careful precision on the top of his laundry hamper, then reached for his sleeping bag and spread it out on the bunk he had told her earlier that she could occupy.

'Goodnight,' she said, slipping into the sleeping bag, giving him only the briefest sideways glance from beneath the fall of her blonde hair. 'Again.'

The minute she settled in, she knew she had made a terrible mistake. The intimacy of sequestering herself inside Ben's sleeping bag was positively jolting. She could smell the faint citrusy odour of his aftershave, the woodsmoke of a hundred previous camp fires, and something uniquely and essentially Ben. The combined scents assailed her with every breath she took. If there was any way she could gracefully have changed her mind and opted for the scratchy old army blanket, she would have done it. But Ben had pulled it across the bunk and was spreading it out at that very moment. Sighing, Jess rolled on to her side facing away from him and tried to ignore him. She ought to be able to with the light out.

But it wasn't easy. A few seconds later, she heard the clink of his belt buckle as he unfastened it, then the quiet rasp of his zipper going down. The soft sound of denim sliding down his legs and landing on the carpet with a muted thud made her shiver.

She flipped over, irritated, and immediately regretted it. In the next burst of lightning she saw a pair of taut, muscular buttocks in tight blue briefs and a pair of equally muscular, hair-roughened thighs less than a foot from her eyes. She shut them tightly, hoping to heaven he wasn't going to sleep in the nude.

Tonight, at least, he didn't.

Wincing at the sudden crack of thunder that followed the lightning, Ben slid under the blanket, then grumbled something unintelligible. Jess watched him twist around, trying to find a comfortable spot.

The lightning flickered again, the thunder boomed distantly but ferociously. The rain buffeted the camper, the high winds rocking it where it sat. Ben writhed on his mattress.

'For heaven's sake,' Jess whispered, 'go to sleep.'

'Can't,' Ben muttered.

'Why?' Her curiosity was getting the better of her.

'A lot of reasons,' Ben said shortly, flipping over again on his mattress.

'Not used to sleeping alone?' she taunted.

He lifted up on one elbow, staring across at her in the dim, flickering light. 'Are you offering, then?'

'No,' she said quickly. 'Just curious.'

'Remember what curiosity did to the cat. It could have an effect on you, too.'

'I'll keep it in mind.' She tried for a far lighter tone than she felt.

'Do that.' He flipped over again. And again. And again.

Obviously not a man for stormy weather, Jess thought with a glimmer of satisfaction. At least something could disconcert him, even if she couldn't. Good.

Ben muttered again, and Jess smiled. She wondered if he would get any sleep at all tonight. She wondered why she even cared. Let him lie awake and think. Let him count his sins. It would serve him right.

CHAPTER FIVE

JESS AWAKENED SLOWLY, coaxed into consciousness by the noisy tap-tap of woodpeckers, the shrill call of blue jays, and the high-pitched chatter of the children at the next campsite.

For a few minutes she didn't even move. She just lay there, cocooned in Ben's sleeping bag, luxuriating in its cosy warmth and the faint musky smell that brought Ben immediately to mind.

She hoped that it had been desensitising her while she slept, so that today she would be on a more even keel emotionally where Ben Standish was concerned. She turned her head and looked over at his bunk apprehensively. But Ben was nowhere to be seen.

Her split second of disappointment turned quickly to relief. Taking advantage of his absence, she had a shower and washed her hair, then brushed it and braided it into one long plait down her back. Her jeans were still damp, but she had no doubt the ones in the tent were damper, so she struggled into these. But she drew the line at putting on her still wet shirt, instead opting for Ben's. Leaving the last two buttons undone, she knotted the tails together at her midriff. There would be time enough when they were actually in White Birch Bay to tuck them in so the mosquitoes wouldn't eat her alive.

She had just gone outside and had crawled into her soggy, sagging tent to retrieve her pack when she heard footsteps behind her.

'Can I give you a hand?'

She poked her head out to see Ben coming up the trail towards her. He wore jeans and a forest-green polo shirt that picked up the haunting emerald highlights in his tawny eyes. There were dark circles beneath them, and she thought her notion of how little sleep he would get must have been accurate. But it didn't seem to have slowed him down much.

He came towards her with an easy grace that proved how much time he must spend in the woods. Her heart, she decided, must be beating faster than his. Because it was hammering. The desensitisation hadn't worked.

Without waiting for her answer, he bent to help her, gathering up her gear quickly and efficiently and stowing it in the camper. She kept waiting for him to continue his campaign of innuendo, but he was silent until he said, 'We can have a light breakfast on the road, if you don't mind. I want to get moving.'

'Fine with me,' said Jessica, because it was. She had no desire to dilly-dally around with Ben Standish. The quicker they could get to White Birch Bay, the quicker she could get to work. In an undeveloped area like that, she would need all her wits to camp and cook and watch for wolves and any other significant natural occurrences. There, she was certain, the problem of Ben Standish would not loom insurmountably. He would be just one among many. Like mosquitoes. And deer flies.

She settled herself in the passenger seat and contented herself with watching the scenery as Ben drove. Ben was silent, which was just as well. Talking to him was a bigger strain then simply sitting there, even if every moment that she did so, a dozen questions popped into her head that she wanted to ask him. Questions about her mother. About what had happened. About—there were too many things, all of them painful. She wouldn't ask. She couldn't. It was better just to leave things alone.

They drove on two-lane highways through thick conifers and birch forest, each apparently preoccupied with his and her own thoughts for the better part of the morning. Then, without warning, Ben tossed her a map.

'We'll be getting there soon,' he told her. 'Figure out how, will you?'

'Sure.'

Maps she could figure out. Wolves she could figure out. It was Ben Standish who was the mystery—what he wanted, how to deal with him. Don't think about it, she told herself. Just read the map.

She did, directing him to turn off the highway on to a narrow country road that cut through the forest, bisected a tiny somnolent town, and ultimately reached a dead end at a cable stretched across the road not far from a row of summer houses that skirted the shore of Lake Michigan.

'You could drive around the cable and follow that road.' She pointed out a narrow double-rutted trail that would take them closer to White Birch Bay.

Ben shook his head. 'I'm not breaking an axle on that. This is the end of the line.' He pulled the camper over to the side and cut off the engine. Taking the map from her, he frowned down at it, then shrugged.

'It's only about five or six miles along the shore. Surely you can hike that.'

'Of course I can hike it!' Jessica bristled.

'Well then . . .'

'Can you?' Her voice was scathing.

Ben smiled. 'Watch me.'

It certainly wasn't an experience for everyone, Jessica thought half an hour later as she trudged marsh bog, her heavy, still wet pack weighing her down, the sweat making rivulets through the mosquito repellent as it rolled down her forehead and demanded that she blink it back.

The sun was beating directly down on her, and the mosquitoes were attacking her lotioned body with an enthusiasm that made her think she had simply doused herself with an insect equivalent to *béarnaise* sauce. Just ahead she could hear the soft sound of waves breaking on the shore. Thank heavens. There would be fewer mosquitoes there.

She had forgotten the deer flies.

'Damn!' She slapped one that refused to budge from her nose. It died obligingly and she lumbered on.

'Hey, wait up!' she heard Ben call from somewhere behind her.

Ignoring her, she plodded on. She hadn't waited for him to get his stuff together, had simply grabbed her backpack and had taken off. Ben had had to assemble his camera gear, put together a pack from the assorted paraphernalia in his camper, and then secure the vehicle. It had given her a head start for which she was obliged. In fact, she was surprised he was so close already. He must be in better shape than she thought.

While she was wondering about that, he caught up with her, lifted his camera and took several shots in rapid succession.

Jessica scowled, then stuck her tongue out. 'What are you doing?'

'Shooting you?' Ben offered. 'It's my job, remember?'

'To shoot the expedition.'

'To shoot the biologist.'

'Working.'

'You are working.'

'I suppose so,' she said. 'But it doesn't feel like work.' Even though she found the bugs annoying and the sweat irritating, there was still a feeling of happiness welling inside her. Just being out in the woods was enough to do that for her. It was from all her early exposure to the perils of the 'civilised' world, she suspected. Clarissa's world had made mosquitoes look good. But she didn't expect Ben to understand that.

So she was surprised when he fell into step beside her and said, 'I know what you mean. There's a peacefulness here. A rightness you don't get many other places.'

Jess shot him a sceptical glance. But then, without wanting to, she recalled that this man had once sloughed through oil slicks and sloshed through heavy surf without complaining before he had given it up for glamour and Hollywood parties. But however hard she stared at him, he didn't blink. He seemed to mean precisely what he said.

She remembered how distasteful Kyle thought her wilderness work was and wished that Ben would turn out more like him. It wasn't fair that a man who was so right in this way could in fact be so wrong for her.

'Do you really think you're going to spot any wolves?' he asked her now.

'I hope so.'

'You do?'

'Don't sound so surprised.'

'I am. I thought the company hiring NRRI didn't want wolves up there. It would sure as hell mess up their development plans, wouldn't it?'

'Of course. But they just want to know the facts. That's why they hired us. They don't want to invest in territory where there are wolves.'

'Because the wolves will eat everyone up?' said Ben, grinning.

'No. Because it will cause a fight between developers and wildlife enthusiasts. Fights cost money. It has nothing to do with wolves. Wolves don't attack people. It's just that everyone believes they do. Wolves get very bad press.'

'They need a PR man.'

'Probably. The misconceptions about them positively amaze me.'

'You amaze me,' Ben said quietly, slowing his pace, looking at her with his intent golden hazel eyes.

Jess stopped, her heart suddenly thudding. She brushed a deer fly off her cheek. 'How so?'

A tiny grin quirked the corner of his mouth. 'Specialising in wolves, I guess. I can't figure it.'

She scowled. 'Why not?'

'You're a beautiful woman. Gorgeous, actually. You could be doing any number of other, more glamorous things.'

'Glamour doesn't interest me.' Jess started walking again.

'And wolves do?'

'Yes.'

'Why?'

'Because wolves are faithful, for one thing. They're committed to each other, to their pack. They're affectionate with each other and with their pups. They take mates for life. And,' she added sharply, fixing him with a glare that dared him to contradict her, 'based on my experience they have a damned sight more to recommend them than most people do!'

Ben winced, the arrow hitting home, and Jess saw a faint reddish tinge colour his cheeks.

'You could be right,' though, was all he said as he walked on. But Jess was convinced that she had made her point. At any rate, he didn't seem to want to pursue the conversation any further.

When they reached the lakeshore, the going got easier and less insect-ridden. Right at the edge of the water, the sand was hard-packed and easier to walk on. Ben picked up his pace, but Jessica found no reason to hurry. She could hardly expect to see any wolves bounding in and out of the creeks that poured into the lake, but she could at least look for tracks. Also, it put some space between herself and Ben.

So she dropped back, pausing to check the mouths of the creeks that spilled icy reddish brown water into the deep blue lake. She found some paw prints. Raccoon, deer, rabbit, but not wolf.

By the time she reached the edge of the White Birch Bay area, Ben had already pitched his tent. Until that moment she had held out the fond but not very likely hope that he would be hiking back to his camper each night to sleep. Guess again, Watson, she told herself. There was going to be no respite at all.

She couldn't help thinking, however, that he looked right at home as he gathered stones to surround the shallow fire pit he had dug. He moved easily and with the assurance of lots of practice. At least he wouldn't be the problem that the only other photographer she had taken on assignment had been. That man had worn dress shoes and a short-sleeved shirt. Between his blisters and his bites, he had complained every second. Jess knew Ben wouldn't do that.

A tiny part of her wished he would. Then she could be happier about rejecting him. It was hard to keep remembering how unsuitable he was when he strode up to her, hands outstretched, saying, 'Give me your gear and I'll spread it out to dry while you map out your plan for ferreting out the wolves.'

Before she could object, he was helping her off with her pack and unzipping it. She flexed her shoulders, grateful to be free of the burden, almost grateful to Ben himself. Then she blanched when she looked over to see him draping her very serviceable, but decidedly feminine, underthings over nearby low-hanging branches. The colour rose unbidden in her cheeks, but she bit her tongue and didn't protest. It was best to let him think it didn't matter to her. Heaven knew what errant thoughts would go through his head if she made a fuss!

'I'm going to follow this creek a way inland,' she told him. 'Just a preliminary check.'

'I'll be right with you.' He finished draping the rest of her clothes, then fished through his camera bag, taking out his Nikon and looping the strap round his neck. He tucked a couple of spare lenses into the ample pocket of his shirt and then stood up. 'All set. You ready?'

As she would ever be, Jess thought. This is what you're here for, fool, she told herself severely. This is your job. Just get on with it. And let Ben get on with his. She led the way, keeping her eyes down, studying the edges of the narrow creek bed for any sort of animal tracks. She moved slowly, patiently, trying to think like a wolf or a raccoon. But all the while she was terribly conscious of the man dogging her footsteps and the occasional click of his camera as they went.

The mosquitoes increased as they moved inland, and Jess slapped at them irritably. Ben slapped, too, but made no comment.

Finally she stopped and looked at him almost quizzically. 'You know, you amaze me too,' she blurted before she could stop herself.

'How so?'

'You don't seem to mind any of this.'

'I don't, really. The advantages outweigh the drawbacks.'

Jess wasn't sure what advantages he meant and wasn't sure she wanted to ask. So she simply added, 'I thought you liked a more glamorous world.'

'No. Glamour doesn't interest me much either.'

'It did.'

'Yes, once,' he admitted. 'But people change, Jessica.'

Do they? she wondered. Or was it simply wishful thinking, a way of making uncalled-for feelings acceptable again? She slapped away another squadron of mosquitoes about to land on her arm and walked on, trying to sort out her thoughts.

'What made you change?' she challenged him finally.

He had been walking behind her, in the age-old single file of the wilderness. But when she asked her question, his hand came out and caught her by the shoulder, stopping her in her tracks and turning her so that she was looking up into his face.

'Do you really want to know?' he asked bluntly, his expression sceptical.

Did she? Jess licked her lips, then took a deep breath and squared her jaw determinedly. Why not?

'Yes,' she said roughly, 'I think I do.' And let's see if you can convince me, was the unspoken message she sent with her words.

Ben nodded briefly, as if accepting her challenge. He started walking again, keeping pace with her through the thick bed of conifer needles. 'I owe it all to you,' he said lightly.

Jessica stopped flat. 'What?'

He lifted one dark brow and gave a quick, almost apologetic shrug of his shoulders. 'I do,' he said simply. Then, taking her arm, he pulled her along to walk with him again.

Jess could have been walking over sabre-tooth tiger tracks for all she was paying attention to the ground she was supposed to be watching then. She was staring at Ben, trying to figure out what was going on inside his head. It was not unlike the sort of speculation that had gone into the background work for her Master's thesis. Then she had spent a winter tracking wolves near Lake Superior, studying their family structure and, quite naturally, trying to fathom the reasons behind their patterns of behaviour. Just as she was trying to fathom Ben now.

'Me?' she echoed finally, an obvious edge of disbelief in her response.

'You.' He continued walking, following the curve of the quietly moving water. He opened his mouth to speak, then thought better of it, shoved a hand through his hair, rumpling it, then jammed the hat he had been wearing back on to his head. It gave him a sort of rakish Indiana Jones look that was disgustingly appealing, and Jessica deliberately looked away. 'I found out that glamour wasn't all it was cracked up to be.'

'Really?'

'Life in the fast lane can be fun,' he went on carefully, as if testing each word to see if it would explode as he spoke. 'It's flashy, funky, demanding. And it has its costs.'

'Tell me about it,' Jess said sarcastically.

Ben shot her a wry glance. 'I don't need to, do I?'

Jess shook her head and kept walking, supremely conscious of his hand on her arm.

'Well, I wish somebody had told me about them,' he said. 'But, hell, I probably wouldn't have listened anyway.'

'What do you mean?'

'There are some things nobody can tell you. Some things for which experience is the only teacher.'

'And Clarissa taught you well.' Jessica's voice was both knowing and bitter.

Ben grimaced. 'I suppose so. But Clarissa was just the start of it.'

Jess felt an ache beginning somewhere in the region of her heart. She was not at all sure she wanted to hear any more of this. She hadn't got used to even thinking of Ben with her mother after eight long years. She knew for a fact she didn't want to hear about the other women in his life. But before she could speak, Ben went on, 'Anyway, suffice it to say, that sort of life isn't all it's cracked up to be. It makes you hollow, empty. You get fame and fortune at the expense of gossip; parties, backstabbing, more parties. There's nothing of value there. Nothing at all.'

'No,' Jess agreed. She had spent the earliest years of her life in that very lifestyle and she knew he was right. She was just surprised he knew it.

Ben's mouth twisted. 'And then there was you.'

She looked at him, perplexed and astonished. What was he getting at?

He took her hand and dragged her over to sit on a fallen log, half buried in the forest floor. 'It didn't happen all at once,' he told her, 'this sense of purposelessness, this wandering. I mean, when you've been sleepwalking as long as I had been, it takes a while to wake up.'

He shifted around on the log so that they sat side by side, their clasped hands resting on his thigh. Jess looked at their intertwined fingers and took a deep breath, trying to concentrate on what he was saying.

'I was drinking more and thinking less. But when I did think, I began to wonder what I was accomplishing, what the heck I was doing all day shooting pictures of beautiful plastic people through Vaseline-edged lenses. I wanted to do something different, something that made me feel alive. But I couldn't think clearly enough to figure out what it was.' He shook his head, dark hair falling across his forehead as he stared down at the carpet of needles between his boots.

Jess didn't say a word.

'And I might never have figured it out if I hadn't agreed to shoot a "bear country nude layout" in Big Bear,' he told her, slanting a faint, almost sheepish grin at her.

Jess felt her heart nudge her ribs. 'A "*bear* country" nude layout?' She narrowed her gaze. 'Which kind of *bare?*'

He laughed. 'Precisely.' He shoved the hat back on his head and scratched his nose. 'Four nubile young beauties and a baby black bear from some better-left-unnamed zoo.'

'What happened?' Jess was intrigued in spite of herself.

'We were on location in the woods, and, as you might guess, we had attracted a fair share of interested sightseers . . . '

Jess could well imagine. 'And?'

'One of them had a springer spaniel who dug up a nest of cottontail rabbits while his master was—er—sightseeing.'

Jess frowned. 'So?'

'So he killed the mother before anyone could stop him. But the babies lived.' He paused and stared out into the creek that swept past their feet. 'There were four of them. Just barely had their fur. Tiniest things you ever saw.' His voice was filled with repressed emotion. He sighed heavily and shook his head, remembering. 'The general notion was that we ought to toss them in the lake and be done with them.'

Jess swallowed. 'What *did* you do?'

He turned his head and met her questioning stare. 'I remembered you and the pelicans.'

Her heart did a somersault in her chest.

'I didn't let them kill the litter. In fact I stopped the whole damned shoot while I wrapped them in my jacket and took them back to my cabin. I got a lot of razzing for it, actually. They were known as "the playboy's bunnies". But I didn't give a damn. I spent the next few weeks learning how to keep them alive. I've got a lot of experience with parenthood.' He gave her a wry grin, then stretched out his feet in front of him so that the heel of his hiking boot was almost in the creek. 'And while I was doing it, I thought a lot about you. About that summer—' and the look in his tawny eyes challenged her to think about it, too '—and about what really mattered in life.'

'And what did you decide?' Jess's voice was a bare whisper.

'That it was time to get my life back on the track, to rediscover what I really wanted and the values I'd left behind. That's when I left LA.'

'And moved to Missouri?'

'No. That took a couple of years, actually. I just moved around, camped out. Backpacked. Got in touch with nature again. With myself. I started taking photos again—real ones this time. No Vaseline, no sequined ladies.' He smiled. 'I got back to basics, I guess. The basics have become very important to me.'

His words hung between them, half pledge, half challenge. And Jessica, looking into his eyes, saw something very basic within them—a spark, a need, a flame of desire so elemental that, without her wanting it at all, an answering flame flickered to life within her.

A force as strong as it was invisible drew his lips towards hers. 'Like this,' he whispered just a split second before their mouths touched.

And Jessica, drawn in, thought, yes, like this. For it was not at all unexpected. Like last night's storm, it had been building between them since the last kiss. But whereas the storm of the previous night had blown itself out in a high-winded fury, theirs was still to come.

And come it did.

Warm and hard, soft and persuasive, Ben's lips brushed longingly, demanded urgently, then withdrew to tease gently again. At their touch, Jess's mouth opened. Her hands came up of their own accord and wrapped around his back, stroking the smooth cotton, feeling the flex of his muscles as his arms lifted and came around her.

Her split second of wonder and struggle against the power of his kiss turned without warning into willing compliance. She had wanted him for years. As far as that went, nothing had changed. And both of them knew it. It was time, she thought with the last clear thought she was capable of, to see if all this attraction was simply adolescent imagination or something more.

Would he move her heaven and her earth as he had once before?

By the time their hearts thundered and their breathing grew ragged, Jessica had her answer.

She was in trouble, deep, deep trouble. There was nothing adolescent about these feelings, nothing adolescent at all.

As she drew back she could still see flames leaping in Ben's eyes, still taste his lips against hers. And, trembling, she wondered if she had weathered the storm or had simply walked straight into the hurricane's eye.

'Jess—' Ben looked serious, his brows drawn together, a fine line between them.

'No! Don't say anything!'

'But—'

'Really. I have to think. *Please.*' The more seconds that separated her from the reality of that kiss, the more agitated she was becoming. You idiot! she chastised herself. What were you doing? Remember who this is! Remember where he's been and all the women he's kissed!

She rose jerkily to her feet. 'I want to go back.'

Ben stood up. 'All right.'

'No. I want to go alone! To be alone.' She left him, almost stumbling over a rock, hurriedly following the creek bed towards the lake. Her shoes slipped on the weeds as she went, her mind tumbling and whirling like the eddies in the small pools into which the creek spilled briefly on its way to the shore.

She didn't stop until she had reached the broad sandy beach. Then she flung herself down and wrapped her arms round her knees and stared out across the lake.

When she had been a child, she had found nothing as comforting as sitting on the seashore. Beside the immensity of the ocean, with its unchanging ebb and flow, all of Jessica's petty emotional upheavals seemed to fade into insignificance. Going to sea in her father's boat had eventually given her some perspective on what had happened between herself and Ben.

But if it had worked once, it didn't seem to be working now. The feelings that his kiss had unleashed within her loomed and threatened. Jessica wrestled with them, trying to subdue them or at least control them.

It wasn't as if she had never been kissed. But she had never kissed like that. She had never felt that urgency, that throbbing ache that still pulsed within her, that made her feel empty at the same moment that she felt that only Ben could fill her emptiness.

And in the cool clear light of a waning Michigan afternoon, that thought frightened her more than she wanted to admit.

In all the world, he was the last man, even including Kyle Walters, with whom she wanted to be involved. Even though the chemistry between them was basic and undeniably volatile, she still did not want it.

But...

But she still felt something for him. God, if only she knew whether he was telling the truth. If only she could trust him. What if he meant it about sorting his life out, about trying to get back to basics? What if he had nurtured the bunnies, wandered the world and thought about her?

Could it be true? Had Ben Standish changed? Or was it just a line, something designed to get him the women he wanted now? But even if he had changed, was that reason enough to forgive and forget all that had gone before? Was it reason enough to give in to this overwhelming attraction and get involved again? Was it worth the risk of being hurt?

No, it wasn't.

Not yet anyway. And certainly not on the basis of a kiss, a promise and an afternoon's re-acquaintance. She needed time. She needed to know him better, to understand him.

If he had really changed, she thought, two weeks of continual living in each other's pockets would prove it to her. She would do more than check out wolf sightings over the next couple of weeks, she decided. She would use the time to check out Ben Standish as well.

She leaned back on her elbows and stretched her feet out before her. With time would come other opportunities, opportunities that Ben's kiss only hinted at.

She prayed she would have the self-discipline to refuse to check them out as well.

CHAPTER SIX

BEN WAS a long time coming back.

Jessica took a brief bath in the lake to wash off some of the day's grime and to cool her overheated blood, keeping one eye on the dunes all the while. Thank heavens, Ben didn't appear. She dried off and dressed again in a pair of stiff jeans and a long-sleeved, cotton chambray shirt, replaited her hair, and stuck a fisherman's hat on her head.

Then she started a fire in the pit Ben had dug, and was just sorting through her supplies in search of something to fix for their evening meal when she saw him amble out of the woods not far from the creek. His hat was pulled down over his forehead and his camera obscured his face from view. She couldn't see him at all.

He, however, was looking directly at her through the viewfinder. Jess scowled at him. He ignored the scowl, continuing to snap pictures undeterred. Eventually she went back to her meal preparation. It wouldn't do to let him see how he could discomfit her. But she couldn't help feeling self-conscious, especially after the intimacy of their last encounter. She grew warm just thinking about it.

But Ben threw iced water on her thoughts by tipping his hat back and saying casually, 'By the way, I forgot, I need you to sign a release form.'

'A what?'

'Release. You're in a lot of these photos. I can't publish them without your permission.'

'Oh.' A shudder went through her as she remembered those other photos—the ones of her mother.

She could never tell him of the pain she had experienced when she had opened that magazine Sarah had given her and had seen those provocative photos of Clarissa. Had Ben tricked her mother into giving her consent? She would never know. Besides, it wasn't the same thing, she told herself. This was a job and nothing else.

'Give it to me,' she said dully.

He went to the tent and re-emerged a few moments later with a paper that he thrust in front of her. She read it, trying to find some reason not to sign it, but there was none. It was all straightforward. She could imagine what Gunnar would say if she balked. Fishing a pen out of her pocket, she scribbled her name.

Ben's camera clicked. She scowled at him.

He shrugged, grinning. 'An historic moment. It's my job, after all.'

'Just remember that,' Jess said gruffly.

He lowered the camera slowly, golden-flecked eyes peering at her above it. 'I'll keep it in mind,' he drawled. He crossed the campsite, lifted the flap of his tent and set the camera down inside. 'And, Jess?'

'What?' She looked up warily from the packet of Stroganoff she was emptying into the pot.

'You keep that kiss in mind, won't you?'

As if she wouldn't, she thought much later as she lay sleepless in her tent that night. As if she could think of anything else at all.

She hadn't deigned to answer his remark, but she knew—and he knew—that it had struck home. They moved in a tense silence for the rest of the evening.

Jess had done her best to ignore him, needing the distance, busying herself by going over the detailed ordinance maps of the area, trying to get a mental map in her head before she headed out tomorrow at dawn to look for any signs of wolves.

But though she tried, her mind would only stay partially concerned with the wolves. More often than she would have liked, she found herself glancing up to the spot where Ben sat on a blanket across the campfire, fiddling with his cameras, then setting up a tripod and taking a few time exposures of her as she worked.

But, 'Hold still,' was all he said to her when, once, she had looked as if she was going to move.

It was most unsatisfactory, she thought, and it wasn't telling her anything about him that she wanted to know. Except, perhaps, that he was dedicated to his work.

But, short of sitting down and asking him a million impertinent questions which tongue-tied her just to think about, she had to be satisfied with that. She was relieved when he put the camera away. She did the same with the maps and stood up and stretched, announcing, 'I'm going to bed.'

'Good idea,' Ben said mockingly, but she rebuffed the remark with the silence it deserved.

Jessica just wished now that she could put him out of her mind. Think about wolves, she told herself. But thinking about wolves brought wolves to mind. It brought her visions of soft fur, loping gaits, and tawny green and gold-flecked eyes.

And she was right back thinking about Ben again. She groaned and thumped her jacket into a more satisfactory lump beneath her head.

She heard Ben kick dirt on the fire. Then he rustled around in his tent and she saw the faint flicker of his flashlight before he extinguished it, and there was total silence from across the way. That was almost more provoking than hearing him move around. It gave her more time to think, to wonder about the Ben of eight years ago and the Ben of today. Both of them danced through her thoughts, taunting her, tempting her. Which was the real one? Was he the same or had he changed? Could she trust him this time? How could he ever have run off with her mother?

Three hours later she was as wide awake as she had been when she first lay down.

She tried to tell herself that it was often like this the first night of an expedition. It took time to get used to sleeping outdoors, to get over the first enthusiasm for the study, to put things in perspective. And it did, of course. But even she wasn't gullible enough to believe that those were the reasons she was lying awake tonight.

She hadn't spared the wolves half a dozen thoughts in the last three hours. Her mind was totally consumed with Ben Standish, and he was driving her mad.

Finally she sat up and groped for her hiking boots in the dark. Then, pulling on her jacket, she eased up the zipper of her tent. If Ben Standish was going to interfere with her sleep, she might as well get to work right now. There were other ways to hunt out wolves than search out scent markings and wait for sightings in the forest.

She crept out into the darkness, slowly slid the zipper back down, and moved quietly away from the tent. Ben's was between hers and the forest, so she took extra care to move softly as she passed it. She heard no movement from within. He was probably asleep. Anyone with an ounce of sense would be. And she doubted that *she* could evoke the sorts of feelings in him that would keep him awake for long.

She hoped not, anyway, for she had no intention of waking him and taking him along with her. He couldn't take pictures in the dark anyway, she reasoned. So there was no earthly reason to call him. If this worked he would hear it anyway.

They had pitched their tents in the shallow depression between the dune closest to the lake shore and the one that sloped gently back into the forest. It took Jess only a moment to become accustomed to the sliver of moonlight that she had to work with and to edge her way up the slope and into the woods beyond.

There she walked quietly and comfortably between the trees, enjoying the soft, scurrying night sounds, the mild breeze that touched her face, the cool whisper of the leaves in the trees. Following the creek she had walked beside earlier, she made her way inland.

She wasn't sure how far she had walked. Far enough, she hoped, so that if she woke Ben, he wouldn't immediately know it was her. Stopping, she waited, perfectly still, just listening, getting her bearings.

A small animal scuffed in the needles on the other side of the creek. Jessica glanced over, but couldn't see what it was in the dark. It was too dark to see anything. Even looking back the way she had come, everything was black and shadowed, hidden in the denseness of the trees. It was so quiet she could almost hear them growing.

Perfect, she thought, and tipped back her head and howled.

'What in the hell are you doing?' a voice rasped in the darkness almost directly behind her.

Jessica choked, her howl turning into a surprised yelp. 'Ben!'

'Who else?' His voice was dry.

Her heart was hammering, beating its way out of the confines of her chest. 'You frightened me to death!'

'Sorry.' He didn't sound sorry at all. 'What the devil are you up to?'

'I'm howling,' Jessica said flatly, regaining her equilibrium. She rocked her head to one side, listening. Was that...

'Howling?' Ben sounded as if she had lost her mind.

'Shh!' It was. She could hear it, closer than she had hoped. Low and long, then higher and...

'But—'

'Hush, I said.' To emphasise her point she trod heavily on his foot which, she discovered from both the contact and his muffled groan, was clad only in a sock.

'Sorry,' she muttered, and was even sorrier a moment later when his hands came up to capture her upper arms and pull her back against him.

But at least he was quiet, though she could hear the rapid tenor of his breathing right next to her ear and was sure he could hear her own.

But, more important, they could both hear the answering howl. The single low tone was joined by another, higher, then they blended and varied, joined by another and the short staccato yips of a pup, until soon Jess had no idea how many wolves she was hearing in all.

Then gradually it faded, absorbed back into the forest as if it had never been, and they both stood mute and unmoving.

'God,' Ben muttered finally, and his fingers bit into her arm.

Despite his nearness and her still trembling body, Jess smiled. She wanted to sing, to shout, to dance. There were wolves! There were!

It was like an omen, a lucky star.

The howling began again, first singular, then plural. High, then low. And Jessica felt the same primitive satisfaction she always felt when she heard the wolf howl. It brought goose bumps to her arms and sent an icy shiver down her spine, but it wasn't the shiver of fear or horror, but of pleasure and satisfaction.

She had never tried to explain that to anyone before, and she had no intention of explaining it to Ben now. She simply stood and accepted the resonance that the sound struck somewhere deep inside her. And she sensed that Ben was feeling it with her.

For after the sounds died away again, and she expected him to drop his arms and step away, he still stood holding her. Finally, when he showed no signs of moving, it was Jessica who pried his fingers loose and stepped out of the circle of his arms.

Ben exhaled deeply. 'It was beautiful!'

Jess stared at him, amazed. It was not a reaction she had heard often. She almost wondered if he was joking.

But there wasn't the faintest glimmer of a smile on his face. He looked touched emotionally, almost vulnerable.

Jessica blinked.

Sticking his hands into the pockets of the lightweight jacket he wore, he rocked back on his heels. 'Why didn't you tell me you were coming out to do that?'

Jess shrugged awkwardly. 'You couldn't have taken pictures.'

'No, but I'm writing an article too.'

'I know, but...' her voice trailed off. She couldn't think of a plausible excuse, and she had no intention of giving him the real one.

But she suspected he had guessed it anyway, and her suspicions were confirmed a moment later when he touched her cheek. 'Scared of what might happen?'

'No! Of course not. I just thought you were asleep.'

'Uh-huh.'

'I did! For heaven's sake, if you were awake, why didn't you just call out and say you were coming with me?'

'I didn't know what you were doing.'

'You could have asked.'

'I don't often get what I want by asking you,' said Ben, his voice silky.

'You might try it,' Jess retorted waspishly.

'Will you make love with me?'

'What?'

'You heard.'

She had heard—all too clearly. That was the problem. She was suddenly aware again of the cool night breeze striking her suddenly hot face. 'No! Of course I won't!'

'See?'

'It's not the same. It's—'

'I've asked,' Ben told her softly. 'I want you to think about it before you answer.'

And without waiting for her, he brushed past and walked quickly back downstream towards the hollow where their tents lay.

Jess stood still and wanted to howl again, this time in frustration. She paced irritably around the small patch of forest, muttering and harumphing, wishing she had been able to think of something to say. But her mind was blank. Only her emotions overflowed.

At last, thrusting her hands into her own pockets, she followed him. By the time she got back to the campsite, there was no sign of Ben. Either he had crawled directly into his tent and had zipped up the flap or he had walked right on by, for there was no sound at all to indicate that everything she had just experienced was anything more than a dream.

Or a nightmare.

By morning she still hadn't sorted things out. And she wasn't at all sure what she was going to say to Ben Standish. By rights, she thought, he ought to be the one wondering what to say to *her!* But she doubted if he would be. He'd had years to perfect the debonair polish of the sophisticated man, and plenty of women to practise on.

So she was somewhat taken aback when she emerged from her tent and saw him squatting down by the campfire to have him look up and, seeing her, get a disconcerted look on his face.

'Good morning.' He straightened up slowly, unfolding muscular legs in snug blue denim, it seemed, an inch at a time. He stood with his feet spread slightly apart, his stance wary, as if he were wondering about her as much as she wondered about him.

'Good morning,' Jess managed. 'It's a good day for work,' she added, then thought that sounded inane.

'Yeah.' Ben jumped on her comment eagerly. 'I just finished some breakfast. As soon as you have yours, we can get going.'

'I'm not really hungry.'

'Jess.'

She stopped edging away.

'Come have some breakfast.'

'Really—I—'

'I won't bite. I'm not a wolf.'

'More's the pity,' she replied before she could stop herself.

A corner of his mouth lifted. 'What's that supposed to mean?'

She shrugged lightly. 'Wolves aren't promiscuous.'

'Neither am I.'

'Oh?' That was news to her.

Ben scowled. 'Did you think I was propositioning you last night?'

'It sure as hell sounded like it!'

He kicked the dirt with his boot. 'I don't make love to all the ladies, Jess.'

No, just her mother and other assorted lovelies. In the clear light of day she wondered how the heck she could have even considered trusting him again. 'No kidding?' Her voice dripped disbelief.

'No kidding.'

'You're Mr Clean Jeans? Mr Proper Gentleman?'

'Yes,' he said seriously. 'Now.'

Jessica gave him a scornful look. 'Prove it,' she challenged.

He gave her a rueful grin. 'What do you think I'm trying to do?'

She didn't have an answer for that, save for the red that crept up her neck and stained her cheeks as well.

Turning away, she brushed past him, flustered and perplexed. Everything in her world seemed to be turning topsy-turvy. She was certain of only one thing—it was going to be a long two weeks.

IN FACT the time passed more quickly than she would ever have thought possible. Ben did, indeed, seem intent on 'proving it', and made no further mention of making love to her. Although the way he looked at her sometimes, especially when he didn't have a camera in front of his face to hide his expression, told her all too clearly what he was thinking.

Jessica, unfortunately, was thinking about it, too.

In fact she was taken aback and had trouble remembering when Ben dropped down beside her on the dunes one afternoon and asked. 'Are you dating anyone now, Jessica?'

She blinked, astonished at the question coming out of the clear blue and then further astonished that Kyle's name didn't spring to her lips. Of course, she wasn't still dating him, but she hadn't noticed how long it had been since she had even given him a thought. The hurt had healed, she realised. And it had healed in a matter of a couple of weeks. Ben Standish, however, seemed to have the power to touch her profoundly even after years and years. So it was with wariness that she answered him, 'A few men.'

'Nothing serious?'

'I wouldn't exactly say that,' she told him, unwilling to give him any encouragement at all. It wasn't him she feared as much right now as herself. She was enjoying his company again just as she had all those years ago.

She didn't mind when he dogged her every step with his quiet professional persistence. She didn't resent his intelligent questions or the help he offered whenever he thought it might be welcome. He didn't overstep the bounds of respect for her professional knowledge either, deferring to her when things had to be decided about how the study was to be conducted.

It was terribly seductive, she decided. If it hadn't been for the past they had between them, she knew she would most likely have fallen into his arms.

And even there he was getting under her guard.

She found herself wondering how such a coolly competent professional man as Ben Standish could ever have done something so scandalous as run off with her mother. And she couldn't seem to come up with any good solid answers. Youth, she told herself. Infatuation. Love? She didn't know. She wasn't even sure she wanted to know. But she made herself wrestle with the notion over and over again because it kept her from flinging caution to the winds and giving in to the attraction that grew between them every day.

But it was getting harder to look at the man who lay unmoving for an hour at a time on the ground amid sharp pine needles and rocks to get just the right shot of a raccoon fishing a stream or a blue jay feeding its babies and to think of him as the man who had taken those photos of her mother and had spread them all over one of the most widely circulated men's magazines of the day.

But he had. He and his 'Vaseline-edged' lenses. Had he really changed? Or was that just a story he had cooked up for her benefit, a neat way of pulling the wool over her eyes?

Well, she had to admit it was working, because he backed his story with the way he acted everyday. He took plenty of pictures of her, but they were all fully clothed and few of them were the least bit flattering. More often than not he caught her with her face in the dirt or sniffing a rock or a tree.

'I'm looking for scent markings,' she told him irritably, her face red. 'Or sniffing for them,' she qualified.

He managed to keep a straight face. 'Go right ahead.' The shutter clicked again.

Jess had gone ahead. But there were a lot of trees, a lot of bushes, and a lot of rocks. And she couldn't possibly spend the rest of their time there sniffing them all!

But, other than her howl, to which there had been a definite response, she had no real indications of wolves in the area. The weather had been uncommonly dry since they had arrived, so tracks were at a minimum except right around the creek. And, unfortunately, none of the tracks she found there belonged to wolves.

She had paced through a good part of the White Birch area with Ben at her heels, and she had found very little. But that morning she came upon a clearing that had possibilities. The area was obviously stony beneath a very thin layer of topsoil, and no trees were growing there. But there were large boulders nearby and the potential existed, Jess thought, for a wolves' den dug out by the boulders. She had poked around a bit, but there were no wolves about so she had left.

Tonight, however, she intended to go back and do another howl. She had done one more since the first one. It, too, had got a reply, but the wolves hadn't been very close.

Not like Ben. He had been much too close for comfort. He had stood right behind her with his arms wrapped around her 'to ward off the chill', he had said. And when the sound of her voice had finally died out, the two of them had stood locked in the ensuing silence and waited for an answer. When it came, Ben's arms had wrapped her more tightly, and she felt him take a deep breath, his chest pressing against her back.

'Whew!' he had whispered when it was over, and she knew the sounds had shaken him.

She had been shaken herself. Humbled almost. The emotions she sensed in the wolves' howls seemed deep and intense, far more so than human emotions. She surprised herself by saying so out loud.

'I know what you mean.' Ben loosened his arms from around her and stepped back slightly. 'They do seem to feel more.'

Jess turned and looked up at him in the moonlight. An almost melancholy smile turned up one corner of his mouth.

'Except for loneliness,' he said softly. 'I think I know just as much as any wolf does about that.' His eyes met hers, just inches away.

Jess stared, mesmerised, caught in his gaze. She didn't know what would have happened if Ben hadn't finally ducked his head, stuffed his hands in his pockets and walked away.

It was no wonder, then, that she worried about going howling with him tonight. She had teetered on the brink of relieving his loneliness the previous night. Only a superhuman effort had kept her rooted to the ground and unresponding until Ben's smile had finally faded and he had turned and walked away.

Every day she had more good memories of him that were blotting out the earlier bad ones.

That very morning, for example, she had awakened to find him unzipping the flap to her tent.

'What the—'

He poked his head in, grinning all over his face. 'Breakfast in bed.' And before she could say a word, he had crawled in, bringing with him a bowl of instant oatmeal, a mug of steaming hot coffee, and two pieces of toast with peanut butter.

'My heavens,' gasped Jess, astonished. 'To what do I owe the honour? The bread's not even burned!'

'I know.' Ben's smile was smug. 'No particular honour. Just because you're you.'

And that almost choked her right there. She gave him a quick, hunted look and he laughed.

'Relax,' he coaxed. 'I'm not going to take advantage of you.'

But regardless of whether he intended it or not, Jessica felt at a very distinct disadvantage. He was dressed in a plaid flannel shirt and cord jeans; she was wearing a baggy T-shirt and her underwear. Of course, the sleeping bag did protect her somewhat. But psychologically she felt very vulnerable indeed. It was, she decided, an extremely small tent. Never having shared it before, she had had no idea how small. Ben Standish quickly remedied that.

She managed to eat the oatmeal, drink the coffee and nibble one piece of the toast. Ben, with little urging on her part, consumed the other, and was polite enough to leave without her having to say anything when she finished, leaving her to get dressed.

But their intimate breakfast had set the tone for the day, as far as she was concerned. And she was terribly relieved when he opted to stay behind to mess around with one of his cameras while she hiked back into the woods. But then she found the clearing, checked it out, muttered and speculated, and knew she would be howling again that night.

Ben knew it, too, the moment she came back and told him what she had found. 'What time should we go?' he asked her.

Jessica shrugged. 'I don't know.'

She wanted to put it off as long as possible. Another night-time walk through the woods with Ben would be temptation indeed—especially after this morning's breakfast. At odd times during the day she found herself wondering what it would be like to wake up next to him, to share intimate breakfasts like that with him every day. And she was glad when she finally stumbled on to the clearing, because it gave her something else to think about for once.

What she ought to be thinking about anyway, she reminded herself now. 'I'll stop by your tent,' she told him.

She procrastinated as long as she could. She had brought along a scholarly treatise on wolf scent markings, and she tried to tell herself she found it so fascinating that she couldn't put it down. She did, in fact, manage to get through twenty or thirty pages of it. But not without checking her watch every five minutes.

But finally, just past midnight, she could put it off no longer.

'Here goes nothing,' she muttered, mentally cloaking herself in a suit of iron willpower. And she clambered out of her tent and crossed the hollow to Ben's.

Before she could speak, his tent opened and he slipped out.

'A good date is always prompt,' he said softly, falling into step beside her.

Jessica felt her willpower slip an inch. 'Ssh!' she commanded, and turned away, walking briskly into the woods.

Ben shadowed her the whole way, his footsteps even more silent than her own. And he stopped each time almost the very second she did, as if he knew even before she did what she would do.

'Now?' he asked in her ear when she paused beside a tree.

They were no more than fifty yards from the clearing, but Jessica didn't want to go any closer. Too near and she might invade the wolves' space, presuming that there were wolves there.

She nodded, then hesitated, feeling self-conscious and vulnerable. It was the primitiveness of it, she decided, the sound of raw emotion. She didn't want to make those sounds with Ben standing there just inches away. It unnerved her completely.

But then, summoning Gunnar's scowling visage and all her most professional memories of her father, she began. Suddenly she was amazed to hear Ben's deeper voice join hers. His arms wrapped her loosely and, without even realising it, she settled back against the hard wall of his chest, her shyness vanishing, her emotions bending with his. Then, when his hands squeezed hers lightly, they fell silent.

For what seemed an eternity no answer came save the pounding of her heart.

Then, far off, a distant howl began.

Jess sagged, disappointed.

'What's wrong?' Ben demanded.

'I hoped they might be clo—' she began, but her words were cut off by a howl so near that she stumbled and fell backwards into his arms.

'Holy Moses!' he muttered.

They stood, mesmerised, trembling, as the answering wail rose and fell, joined briefly by another, then another. And near the end Jess heard an almost tentative, higher-pitched short yowl. She couldn't help but smile.

'What's that?' Ben whispered.

'A cub.'

His arms hugged her gently, his hips cradled her as she leaned back against him, and Jess never knew exactly when it was that her perceptions began to shift.

But as the wolves' howl ended, her awareness of Ben grew. She felt the solid strength of his arms around her and the primitive need building within her. And when he moved to turn her in his arms, she gave in to him, unresisting.

His lips touched hers, briefly and with great gentleness, and then, gradually, with an unrelenting hunger that set a torch to her own desire.

'Jess. Jess, I want you,' he breathed against her mouth. 'I need you. I've always needed you. Please!' His voice was ragged, aching, and an accurate echo of her own thought and needs.

When he lifted her easily into his arms and began to carry her back through the forest towards their tents, she didn't struggle. She couldn't help herself, couldn't help what she was feeling. She was being seduced by moonlight, by the sound of loneliness communicating its need, by the strong arms that held her, by the almost desperate kisses that he bestowed on her once he set her down outside his tent.

His hands steadied her as her feet hit the sand, and somewhere in the farthest recesses of her mind she told herself that sanity ought to bring her emotions to earth as well.

But there was no such thing as sanity tonight. There was only loneliness, and need, and each other.

'Jess?' His voice shook

Her whole body shook, and she lifted her arms and wrapped them around his neck, loving him, trusting him, believing in him. It was a fantasy come true. And it was all the answer that Ben Standish needed.

He held her against him with one arm while he bent and tugged up the zipper of the tent with the other. Then he held it open for her and, without hesitating, Jess crawled into the tent.

It was small, like hers, and in another place and time would have seemed narrow and confining. But tonight it held the world, the universe. She found his sleeping bag and lay back on it, then reached for him as he knelt beside her. She drew him down, accommodating him, letting herself relax so that his body could mould itself to hers.

The hardness of his chest pressed against her heaving breasts, and the strength of his legs tangled with hers. Jess luxuriated in the feel of his lean body against hers, in the soft pull of his fingers as they lost themselves in her hair. His mouth touched hers, then moved on, pressing light, teasing kisses on her cheeks, her nose, her eyes.

Jess's own hands were far from idle. They had waited for years to know this man. And now they kneaded his back, revelling in the smooth bands of muscle and sinew that they encountered. They traced the line of his spine, then pressed lightly against the small hollow low on his back. She felt him arch against her, and the hard press of his arousal was hot against her thigh.

Lifting himself away with a groan, he fell to unbuttoning her shirt. In his haste he fumbled with the buttons, and Jess covered his shaking hands with her own.

'Let me,' she offered.

'No.' His tone was urgent. 'Please. Jess, I—' He didn't finish. He didn't have to. His tone was enough. She lay back and let him finish it himself. She let him undo the last button and lay open her shirt, let his fingers glide down the valley between her breasts. It felt so right, so perfect, as if she had been waiting for just this moment for years.

In fact, she had been. And it was even more wonderful than she had hoped, more beautiful than she had dreamed. Even in the dark confines of Ben's tiny tent, it was all that she could have wanted it to be.

Ben adored her—with his hands, his mouth, his words. And soon her shirt and jeans and panties had disappeared along with his clothes, and it was just the two of them touching, naked flesh to naked flesh, perfect need to perfect passion. Total, consummate desire.

'Ben! Now!' she whispered, writhing beneath him, her hands clutching his hips and drawing him down to her.

And the control that he had been struggling with, but still barely maintaining, snapped. 'God, yes,' he muttered, and let her guide him so that a moment later their union was complete.

'Ah, Jess!' His voice was agonised, his body trembling, and then he began to move.

Jess moved with him. Her response instinctive, she received him with the welcome she had been saving just for him, the welcome that had been postponed for years. This was Ben, the man she had first loved, the man who had come back to her. Her fingers raked his back as he thrust blindly into her. This was the man she wanted, the man she trusted, the man she loved.

And with that realisation came her release, and she cried out against Ben's sweat-slicked shoulder, then felt him shudder wildly and heard her own name muffled against her hair.

CHAPTER SEVEN

JESSICA COULD REMEMBER adolescent dreams like this one. Dreams of waking wrapped in Ben's arms, dreams of his lean torso pressed against hers, dreams of his slow, even breathing as it stirred the soft tendrils of hair next to her ear.

But this was no dream.

She turned slowly in his arms and pulled back a bit, just enough to be able to look at him clearly in the early light of dawn.

His face was relaxed, almost vulnerable in repose. The harsh angle of his jaw and the taut planes of his cheeks were softened by the dark shadow of whiskery stubble. It was the way she had often imagined him, and Jess smiled, leaning forward to brush her lips lightly against his rough chin.

Ben smiled and mumbled, his arms tightening around her as he drew her close again.

'Want you,' he muttered. And Jess, who also wanted him, laid her head against his chest and wondered about the future of wanting Ben.

In the harsh morning light perhaps she would discover that she had regrets, perhaps she would think of the legions of women—including her own mother—who had shared other mornings with Ben, and perhaps then it would matter.

But she wouldn't think about that now. This was not a dream, this was reality. And, as such, she had no desire to test it. It was far too fragile.

'Please God it will be all right,' she murmured, resting her head against his stomach. Then she closed her eyes and slept once more.

When Jessica awoke again that morning, Ben was gone.

She felt a stab of disappointment discovering herself alone, then realised it might be better that way. What if she had opened her eyes to find him smiling smugly at her, pleased with himself for finally having got what he wanted from her? She wouldn't have been able to bear it. His absence, however ambiguous it was, was infinitely better than that. She poked her head out of the tent, expecting to see him nearby. But Ben was nowhere around.

That, she decided, might well be a blessing, too. It would give her time for a quick dip in the lake without his presence to make her self-conscious. She didn't doubt he would expect to swim with her, and in the clear light of day, she didn't know how to feel about that. Except warm.

Hurriedly she grabbed her clothes and dashed for the water.

It was icy and still as a pond in the mid-morning sun, but it sharpened her senses, honed her thoughts. And after she had grown accustomed to it, she lazed about, paddling. Then she washed her hair, swam a bit and felt much better. If Ben returned looking smug, she felt she could face him now. She could manage detachment now. She was cultivating it, in fact.

She needed bit of armour, needed to hide how much she was coming to love him again if she had been nothing more than a romp in the sack to him.

She dried off briskly, then dressed in a clean pair of jeans and a long-sleeved, pale pink cotton shirt. Then she towelled her hair as best she could and began to comb it.

Untangling its snarls always took ages, and it was while she was sitting on a log near the shore doing it that Ben came back.

He appeared on a dune a way down the beach from her, camera slung about his neck, as he stood for a moment at the crest, still unaware of Jessica. Instead he took a picture of a freighter on the horizon. Then he turned and almost casually walked toward Jessica and the camp.

The sight of him made her recognise just how much of her supposed detachment was nothing more than a figment of her imagination. All it had taken was one glance at him and her heart began to race, her palms grew damp, and a lump the size of a pine cone lodged in her throat. For all the detachment she might be able to pretend, she knew that if he was smug and self-satisfied, if she meant nothing to him at all, she could not help being hurt once again.

She licked her lips in apprehension, wondering what she should do. Ignore him? Smile at him? Stand up and wave? Run in the opposite direction?

No, not that, she decided. It was time to stand her ground no matter what. So she stayed where she was, brushing her hair and feigning unconcern, while all the time her heart was doing press-ups inside her chest as she watched him approach.

Ben didn't acknowledge her either until he was within a few feet of tripping over her. Then he stopped and offered her a tentative smile, one not smug at all.

Jess breathed again.

'Hi,' he said.

'Hi yourself.' She offered him a tentative smile of her own.

He looked down at her, and she saw him run his tongue quickly over his lips. Then, when she didn't look away, he dropped down beside her and took the comb from her unresisting fingers, drawing it gently through her hair.

A shiver ran down Jessica's spine.

'God, you're beautiful.' His words were spoken as softly as the faintest breeze. The comb through her hair was subtly erotic, alerting her senses, teasing them. And when moments later it was replaced by Ben's fingers, she dropped all pretence of detachment and turned to wrap her arms around him.

This time she felt everything with an even greater intensity than she had the night before. Now she could see his face, could watch his eyes grow dark with desire and note how his jaw tightened. She could lie back on the sand and glory in his weight over her, could feel the way his need matched her own as they came together urgently and desperately, then collapsed replete with loving, their galloping hearts gradually slowing once more.

This time when Ben grinned at her, she didn't care if he looked smug. She felt more than a little smug herself. She had seen how much he needed her. She had heard his words of want and desire. She had watched his face and body strain in the throes of passion. And she knew that she had satisfied him.

'Whew!' he whispered, the grin still lurking at the corners of his mouth, as he rolled on to the sand beside her, still touching her, his naked body still warm and damp against her own.

'Wow,' Jess corrected, smiling herself. She could scarcely believe the way all those hesitancies had built up into one urgent moment. They had hardly had time to shed their clothes, the need had built so quickly.

Ben leaned over and kissed the tip of her nose, then brushed his lips over her eyelids. 'I think we ought to celebrate.'

Jess gave him a quizzical look.

'How about taking the day off? Going to Mackinac? I've got quite a lot of film to develop and a friend of mine has a business there where I can do it. But apart from that, we could just take a break. What do you say?'

She said yes.

'But,' she added, 'I would like to nose around that clearing a bit before we go. The wolves were there last night. Maybe today I can find some evidence.'

It wasn't what she really wanted at all. For the first time in her adult life, she would willingly have forgone an afternoon of wolf-tracking for an afternoon out with a man. As long as the man was Ben. But without the wolf job, there would have been no second chance for Ben and herself. She owed them that much, then, at least.

'Fair enough,' said Ben. 'We owe them.'

And Jessica smiled at this echo of her own thoughts. It was an omen, she decided. A sign that she had been right to give in last night. This Ben Standish was a different man from the one who had run off with her mother. He had changed, thank God.

The rest of the morning seemed equally blessed. A close examination of the clearing revealed two wolf scats. Jessica was delighted. If she could manage a confirmed sighting now—especially of pups, that would clinch things.

Pleased, she thought the only thing that could improve matters would be to find a nice motel room with a hot bath. But when she said so to Ben as they were hiking out to the camper, he had another suggestion.

'My friend Neil lives on the island. I'm sure he'll let you use the bathtub.' He gave her an appraising, hungry look. 'Wish I could join you,' he growled.

Jessica blushed. But she mumbled, 'Me, too,' quite honestly, and Ben, disarmed by her candour, laughed aloud and crushed her against him, kissing her hard.

'You are the most gorgeous woman,' he told her, and while Jessica knew he was prejudiced, she wasn't averse to hearing him say it, especially since he had seen plenty other more lovely women, she was sure.

They drove across the upper peninsula to St Ignace in a little less than two hours, then boarded the ferry to Mackinac Island.

The island, with its lack of motor vehicles and its nineteenth-century clapboard buildings, would have

enchanted Jessica enough on its own. But comple-
mented by Ben Standish, attentive and loving, it was
the next thing to paradise.

Their first stop was Neil Prudhomme's photography shop. Neil, who had gone to photography institute with Ben in California before returning to the
upper mid-west, did a general photography business. But in the summer the bulk of his work seemed
to be taking old-fashioned photos of tourists who
dressed up in the nineteenth-century costumes he
provided in his shop. There was much giggling and
general mayhem, and he seemed to do a land office
business. He barely had time to show Ben and Jessica to the door of his small white frame house just
behind the shop.

'Of course, it's not really quite as exciting a business as yours,' he told Ben with a teasing grin, 'but
then we can't all photograph luscious ladies.'

'I'm not doing that any more,' Ben said sharply,
scowling, and Neil looked at him warily, then
shrugged.

'Whatever you say. Here's the darkroom.' He
pointed at a door just beyond the kitchen. 'Bathroom with hot running water's just through to the
left. Make yourselves at home. Will you stay for
supper?'

'We'll take you out,' Ben offered.

'I'm sure you'd rather go by yourselves.' His meaning was clear enough, even if he was polite enough not to give Jessica the once-over with his knowing eyes.

'No problem,' Ben said easily. 'We've had each other's company exclusively for the last week and a half.' He was not nearly as polite as Neil, his gaze at Jessica managing to say all the suggestive things they both knew Neil was thinking.

Jess blushed mightily and brushed past them towards the bathroom.

'Take your time,' Ben called after her. 'And if you finish before I do, whatever you do, *don't* open the darkroom door.'

'No fear,' Jessica promised. Not that she wouldn't have liked to. She remembered having had more than one fantasy about Ben and herself in a darkroom all those years ago.

But even she hadn't come up with a fantasy as promising as the one Ben proposed when he opened the door of the darkroom much, much later. He rubbed a weary hand against the back of his neck and flexed his shoulder muscles, then looked up at Jessica, who was sitting on the couch sipping iced tea and thumbing through a magazine and said, 'How about spending the night?'

'Here?'

'No. But there are inns all over the place. As well as the Grand Hotel.'

Jessica's eyes widened. 'Are you asking what I think you're asking?'

'I'm asking *exactly* what you think I'm asking,' he said hoarsely. He went to her and sank down on the couch next to her. 'I want to make love to you all night long. In a bed this time. Just you and me. No wolves. No mosquitoes. No deer flies.'

'No Neil?' she asked softly, smiling.

'Definitely no Neil.' Ben put his arms around her and began kissing her. He pressed her back against the couch, the lean hardness of his body seducing her.

The kiss went on. And on. Finally Ben pulled back, his breathing ragged. 'If I don't quit, there very well might be a Neil,' he said ruefully. 'So—an inn? The Grand?'

Jessica lifted her hand and stroked his cheek, losing herself in the tawny eyes that smiled at her. 'Yes. Whatever you want.'

But first they had to be polite for the rest of the day. Jessica made small talk with Neil between customers while Ben cleaned up. Then they rented bicycles and rode around the town, simply enjoying being tourists together. They found a small bed-and-breakfast inn that Neil recommended, and when Ben registered them as Mr and Mrs Standish, Jessica felt a sharp nervous thrill course through her.

Once they had their rooms, the rest of the day seemed nothing more than a prelude. Their gazes met continually, their hands touched, their bodies grazed one another now and again. It was the slow build-up to a night Jessica was sure she would never forget.

They shared a late supper with Neil at a Victorian restaurant where the food was delicious, and the atmosphere charming. Neil was an engaging conversationalist, and a persuasive one, even getting Ben to agree to take the photos at a small town's Voyageur Days festival the following weekend before they left so he wouldn't have to leave his shop unattended.

'Sure,' said Ben. 'After using your darkroom all day, sounds fair.'

'Thanks. Get some good shots?'

Jessica saw his eyes light up. 'Some beauties.' Even his voice was reverent. She wondered just how good they were.

'Can I see them?' she asked.

'Some time. When I'm getting them together for the article, OK?' He yawned hugely and glanced at his watch.

Jessica smiled when Neil took the hint, pushing back his chair and saying, 'How about a nightcap?'

Ben shook his head. 'No, thanks. We've been in the woods too long. We're both dying for a good night's sleep in a real honest-to-goodness bed.'

Neil grinned. 'Right.'

But Jessica didn't even blush. So what if he knew she was sleeping with Ben? She loved Ben. She had just come to realise that. And she was relatively certain that Ben loved her.

They walked quickly towards the inn as soon as they left Neil at his front gate. Ben's fingers were laced with hers and, if anything, he seemed in more of a hurry than she was.

'I want to kiss you,' he whispered in her ear as they hurried along the dark street.

'What's stopping you?'

'Propriety. If I do, I won't be able to stop. I want you too much. I've wanted you for days. No,' he corrected himself hoarsely, 'I've wanted you for years.'

It was that thought that Jessica held in her mind for the rest of the night while they loved. She knew the feeling. She had suffered from it herself all those years when their lives had taken them in different directions, when she had deliberately learned to hate him. And she was grateful now that things had changed, that they had this second chance.

'Oh, Ben, I love you,' she murmured against his damp shoulder, and she held him tightly and didn't think about anything else. Her mother was in the past. All Ben's naked ladies were in the past. What mattered was the present. And the future.

IN THE MORNING she had what she could only describe as 'honeymoon feelings', as if the world were bright and glorious and she and Ben were among the favoured few. The past had receded, murky and happily forgotten. The future stretched before them, warm and inviting, full of the most wonderful potential that Jessica could imagine.

They walked down to the ferry arm in arm, their minds euphoric, their bodies replete.

'Standish!'

Ben stopped, frowning. There were crowds of people milling by the ferry landing.

'Standish!' the voice called again. 'Is that you?'

He turned then to see a burly man bearing down on them, a cigar jammed in the side of his mouth.

'Torberg.' Ben's voice was flat and unwelcoming, but it made no difference to the man. He wrapped his thick arms around Ben and hugged him tightly.

'You old son of a gun! Where have you been hiding yourself?'

'I'm not in Hollywood any more.'

'Things more lucrative elsewhere, are they?' the man called Torberg chortled.

Ben scowled, not answering. 'Listen,' he said quickly, 'we've got to catch this ferry. Nice to have seen you,' though it was obvious to Jessica that he didn't mean the last bit.

'Hey, not so fast.' Torberg caught his arm. 'I've got a deal for you.'

'Not interested,' said Ben, brushing him away.

But Torberg persisted. 'I'm looking for fresh talent, y'know? Lovely ladies.' He fastened his gaze on Jessica then, assessing her with a look that was half lascivious, half mercenary. She glared back at him, undaunted, even as he added, 'Like this little lady.'

'No!' Ben's voice was harsh.

'Ah, come on,' Torberg wheedled. 'How 'bout it? You could make Little Miss Hicksville a fortune, and one for yourself, too.'

'No,' Ben repeated through clenched teeth.

He jerked his arm away from Torberg and practically dragged Jessica toward the waiting ferry.

Half amused, half annoyed, Jess was only too willing to follow.

'You got my number,' Torberg called after him. 'Just like Clarissa, y'know?'

Jess stopped dead where she stood.

'Come on!' snapped Ben.

'Clarissa?' she demanded. 'Does he mean my mother?'

Ben glared, exasperated, annoyed, angry. 'Come on, Jessica. We're going to miss the ferry!'

'Does he mean my mother?' Her skin crawled at the thought of this man having had anything to do with her mother.

'For God's sake!'

'Does he?'

'Yes, damn it!' The answer came through gritted teeth. 'Now, come on!' He grabbed her arm and hauled her on to the waiting ferry.

'What about my mother?'

'Nothing.'

'How does he know her?'

'Never mind.'

'Ben!'

'I said, *never mind!'* And it was clear from the obstinate line of his jaw that he wasn't going to be coerced into saying another word. The ferry jerked into motion, chugging away from the dock, and Ben looked deliberately away from Torberg, his hands clenching into fists, then relaxing, then clenching again.

Jessica frowned at him, a million questions spinning in her head, none of them with a ghost's chance of being answered. Yet.

She glanced back at the barrel-shaped man still standing at the dock. Obviously he was a part of Ben's past as well as her mother's. Just what part, she didn't know. And didn't seem likely that he would tell her.

Would it always be like this? she wondered. Would there always be people like Torberg stepping out of nowhere to haunt them?

'Look,' Ben said softly, touching her cheek, turning it so she looked directly up into his eyes. 'I'm sorry for snapping at you. It's just that—that—well, I—oh, hell . . .' He rubbed his hand beneath his shirt collar irritably.

'Who was he?'

He shut his eyes and took a deep breath. 'A magazine photographer. A very pushy magazine photographer. Not the sort of man you want to know.'

'But he knows my mother?'

'He likes lovely ladies,' said Ben, his tone mocking. 'You heard the man. He lives in Hollywood.'

'Oh.'

'Anyway, he's not worth bothering with. So forget him. We've got better things to think about.' To prove it, his mouth came hungrily down on hers.

By the time the kiss was finished, Jess had other things on her mind, too. The incident with Torberg was minor, after all. There had to be a million people who knew Clarissa Evans Mallory. Some of them were, undoubtedly, unsavoury or unpleasant. It was just her bad luck to have run into one of them on a day that otherwise might have been paradise.

'Looking forward to getting back to the bay?' Ben asked her as he laid his arm across her shoulders and drew her hard against him.

'I have mixed feelings,' she told him honestly.

He grinned. 'I know what you mean.'

'I do want to find more evidence of the wolves if I can. I only have another week left. But...'

'But for certain things, civilisation has a lot to recommend it,' Ben remarked, and she knew he was remembering last night.

Jessica felt her cheeks burn. But in her mind there was more to it than that. She couldn't help wondering what would happen between them after the expedition was over. Would their relationship be over, too? Or could it last? Did Ben even want it to? She wanted to ask him, but she didn't have the courage. Not yet.

For now she was willing to live day by day, building their relationship bit by bit, taking what came, not dragging out her worries or her questions. Why, whenever questions about the past occurred to her, she squelched them. Their happiness was too fragile to risk ruining over that.

And, as the days passed, she couldn't help feeling she was right. In fact it seemed they were living a Garden of Eden sort of life. Ben was loving, the weather stayed warm but dry, and the wolves cooperated, leaving enough evidence so that she had lots of data to take back to verify their existence.

Early one morning she and Ben even saw them.

There were five of them: two adults, a yearling male, and two cubs about three months old. The two youngest were still awkward and puppylike, given to cavorting in the clearing while Ben and Jessica hovered just out of sight and downwind, hidden by one of the fallen logs that abounded.

They lay side by side, Jess with her binoculars and Ben with his telephoto lens, enchanted while the pups played and the adults occasionally joined in.

'Quite a family,' Ben murmured, snapping a picture.

'Yes.' Jess's eyes never wavered. 'Sometimes I envy them.'

Ben lifted his gaze from the camera to look at her. 'Why?'

She shrugged. 'I wouldn't have minded a little family feeling when I was growing up.'

Ben lay silent for a moment. Then, 'No, I suppose not,' he said softly.

Jess met his eyes levelly. 'I used to think I would rather have been raised by a wolf than a person.'

'And now?'

She smiled, a long slow smile. 'Now I'm reserving judgement.'

He smiled back and leaned over, touching her lips with his. 'Good.'

It was good. The week passed in a haze of golden mornings, clear days and hot passion-filled nights. Jessica had everything she had ever thought she wanted—peace, joy, a few wolves. And Ben.

She tried not to think beyond Friday. She avoided anything that hinted at the uncertainty of their future. Madison could wait. NRRI could wait. Just this once she would hang on to the present. It was enough.

Ben seemed equally reluctant to talk about it. And Jessica didn't know whether she should be pleased or not. He wasn't saying, 'When we're together,' but he wasn't saying, 'When you're in Madison and I'm in Missouri,' either. So maybe when he was officially finished with Jessica and the wolves, he would still be involved with Jessica, the woman.

His actions, if not his words, gave her hope. He was everything she could have wanted—warm, caring, attentive, and every bit as wonderful a lover as she could imagine.

'He's had lots of practice,' she reminded herself darkly before she could stop herself. But just as quickly, she told herself that all his practice didn't matter. It was all in the past. It was the present that mattered now. And *now* Ben was with *her.*

'You want to come with me?' he was asking her now, breaking into her reverie as she sat on the log in the early morning sun and contemplated their last day at White Birch Bay.

'Come with you?'

'To the Voyageur Days,' he reminded her. He patted the camera that he had slung around his neck. 'I promised Neil. Remember?'

She did, but only vaguely. She had been far too caught up in the magic of their day on Mackinac to give much thought to what he and Neil were discussing. She remembered something about him agreeing to take Neil's place somewhere. But now? Today? Their last day?

'Do you have to?' she asked, knowing that she sounded plaintive.

Ben gave her a rueful smile. 'I told him I would. It's a long drive for him, and at the height of the tourist season he really can't afford to be away for the whole day. Why don't you come? We could make a day of it?'

Jessica was torn. A part of her wanted desperately to go with him. But she knew she wouldn't get to spend much time with him really even if she went. Ben on assignment might as well be elsewhere, she had discovered. He was totally consumed by whatever he was photographing. And she suspected that today would be no different. Besides, she really had a job to do here.

She told him so reluctantly, and he obviously didn't like it any more than she did.

'Are you sure?'

'Yes, I was counting on using today to finish up the survey. And I would like one last chance to see the wolves.'

Ben smiled. 'You like the wolves better than me.'

'No,' Jessica assured him. She reached up and put her arms around him, pulling him down and kissing him soundly. I love you, she wanted to tell him. I would give you my heart if you asked for it. But she didn't say anything, because she didn't know if she dared.

Ben met her eyes, his own probing their depths, searching, and Jessica wondered what he was looking for. Then he groaned and pulled her against him, kissing her hard. 'God, why did I ever tell Neil—'

Now it was her turn to smile ruefully. 'I know,' she whispered. 'I know.' She sat back and straightened his collar, then ran her hands down the front of the forest-green shirt he wore. 'You'd better go on,' she told him. 'The sooner you go, the sooner you'll be back.'

Ben's expression was pained, then wry. 'Right,' he muttered, and hauled himself to his feet.

'Tell you what,' said Jess, getting up and beginning to walk with him along the beach as he headed east towards the spot where they had left the camper at the end of the gravel road. 'While you're gone, I'll break camp. That way we'll have more time for—' she broke off, embarrassed to say what they were both thinking.

Ben grinned. 'For each other?'

'Yes.'

'All right,' he agreed. 'But you only have to put things in stacks. I'll do my share of the lugging when I get back.'

'Fair enough.'

He stopped then and put his arms around her again, nuzzling her neck and nibbling her ear, making all sorts of delicious feelings course through her. 'I wish you'd come,' he said.

'I wish you'd stay,' she countered, teasing.

They exchanged an agonised look. Then Jess grinned and swatted his rear end. 'Go on, Standish—hustle! When you get back you'll get what's coming to you.'

He grinned. 'Promise?'

She kissed the tip of his nose. 'I promise.'

She decided to get the drudgery out of the way first. So the minute she got back to their campsite, she began to clean and pack their cooking gear, then doused the fire and covered the pit with sand.

It was a poignant moment, and she felt a hollow ache as she kicked the sand over the ashes, as if she were burying their time together. But that was foolishness. She couldn't expect things to remain like this for ever. They had to move on, change. Even the Garden of Eden didn't last. But she had a feeling they could work something out.

She unzipped their combined sleeping bags, smoothed them out and re-rolled them separately, then dismantled the tent and folded it, laying the aluminium poles alongside the tent next to the cooking gear.

Then, housekeeping finished, she took her notebook and binoculars and headed for the woods. She didn't exactly expect she would get to see the wolves. It was already mid-morning, and the three other times she had seen them it had been quite early or at dusk. But she wanted to try.

The shade of the heavy forest was cool, the sunlight sifting through the trees as she walked briskly but quietly beneath them. She remembered the times she had walked through here with Ben and couldn't help smiling. She was glad, in a way, that she had decided to stay. She had more of him in her mind and her memories than she would have had in the crowds of civilisation.

She moved more cautiously as she approached the clearing, trying to be as silent as possible. The wolves' den, she figured, was dug out beneath a large rock outcropping on the far side of the clearing. Chances were that they weren't there; the cubs were old enough to follow their parents on short daily excursions. But she crouched down behind the fallen log and rested her chin in her hand, waiting and watching just the same.

She had never approached the den directly, not wanting to antagonise the wolves or interfere with their normal behaviour. That wasn't what she was there for.

In any case, she had always been far more apt to want to fit into their sort of life than try to change it! But her chances of being adopted by wolves were slim at best. And anyway, for the past week she had begun to see quite a lot of future in being a human being.

Things were looking bright, she decided. And it was all because of Ben Standish.

It must be fate. She smiled, glad she had jettisoned her first idea of trying for some juvenile revenge upon him for his involvement with her mother. Lately she had even stopped thinking about it. It was past. She was sure now that Ben had grown out of it, even that he regretted it.

It was odd, actually, the way things had turned out, the way her disastrous experience with Kyle had led her full circle until she was once more in love with the man she had first loved all those years ago.

She wasn't sure how long she sat there thinking, remembering, ostensibly watching for wolves. But her wolf-watching at least went unrewarded. They were either gone or in their den. Finally, able to procrastinate no longer, she stood, stretching cramped muscles. She looked back at the clearing as she moved away, recalling the night she and Ben had kissed there, the night they had first made love. A night of wolves and magic and promise.

'Goodbye,' she murmured to her unseen four-footed friends. 'And thanks.'

Back at the shore, she sat down long enough to fill out her survey, listing the animals she did see, then folded it up and stuck it away. Gunnar would be pleased. She had done everything he wanted. And everything *she* wanted as well, she thought with a smile as she set about loading her pack.

It took all of fifteen minutes, then there was nothing else to do but wait for Ben. She paced around the campsite, then made up her mind. If she took a load out to the camper, things would be much further along by the time he got back.

She knew he wouldn't take the camper to the Voyageur Days. That, he had told her earlier, was why he mounted the lightweight motorbike on the back of it. It was fuel-saving as well as more convenient. Especially for Jessica now. Pleased to be doing something, she set to work.

In no time she had her own gear ready to go. And, since they had eaten all the food, she had far less to carry out, so she was able to take some of Ben's gear as well. Then, shouldering her pack and bundling an armload of his clothes against her chest, she set off, whistling, down the beach.

The camper was ferociously hot and stuffy when she arrived. Dumping the pile of clothes on the floor, she set about opening all the windows and doors trying to cool things off. Then she began to put things away.

Her own clothes she left wadded up inside the backpack, only unrolling her sleeping bag on the bunk she had been using before. Then she stopped, realising that she wouldn't be sleeping here tonight. Things had changed since the last time she and Ben had spent the night in the camper.

Smiling, she carried both her sleeping bag and Ben's up to the front where a wide double bunk hung above the seats. Clambering up, she spread them out, then zipped them together.

'Ah, luxury!' She bounced experimentally on the thin foam mattress, then giggled. 'Real luxury.' It wasn't quite the quality of the bed-and-breakfast they had stayed in on Mackinac, but it beat sand, that was certain.

Then, spying the pillows down below that they had left behind, she swung down out of the bunk to get them. 'More high living,' she said, smiling to herself.

'What's this, then?' she muttered when her hand crunched against some stiff paper inside the pillow she had pulled off Ben's bed.

Curious, she reached inside the pillowcase and pulled it out.

Photographs.

Eight-by-ten living colour photographs.

Of Jessica herself.

Nude.

CHAPTER EIGHT

'My God!' Jessica stopped breathing and sat down hard in the passenger seat as if she had been literally knocked off her feet.

She supposed, in fact, she had been. She stared, dazed and disbelieving, down at the photos as her trembling, icy fingers scrabbled through them. She was suffocating again, and this time it had nothing at all to do with stale, stuffy air.

She shut her eyes, willing it all to be a dream—a nightmare—anything but the reality she knew it was the moment she opened her eyes again. A naked, seductive Jessica Mallory stared back at her, enticing and vulnerable.

But never more vulnerable than she felt at this very moment.

Forcing herself to look carefully, she went through the photos again. There were perhaps a dozen of them. And they were very good. Even Jessica, stunned and furious, could see that. They captured her in a state of what she supposed a photographer would call 'primeval naïveté'—an innocent Eve bathing in the Garden of Eden.

Ironic, she thought bitterly, how that image had occurred to her before. Only it seemed she had erred in the casting. Ben had turned out not to be Adam, but the serpent.

'Ben,' she murmured. 'Oh, Ben, no! You didn't!'

But quite obviously he had. Some time when she had been bathing, alone and unaware, she hadn't been alone at all. Ben had been somewhere about, lying low, capturing her on film as she lolled in the water, washed her hair, walked ashore, dried off. Her cheeks burned and she thrust the photos away.

What was it her mother used to say? 'Once a bastard, always a bastard.'

How true. And the appropriateness of quoting Clarissa on the subject of Ben Standish wasn't lost on her either. Not a bit.

What a fool she had been to think he had changed! What a fool she had been to trust him!

And how had he repaid that trust? By taking photos of her that were every bit as compromising as the ones he had taken of her mother!

When would he have tried to sweet-talk her into signing a release for them? she wondered. Then, horrified, she realised that she already had!

The first day he arrived at White Birch Bay he had given her just such a form. It had been intended, of course, for the photos he would take of her in conjuction with the article for *Preservation,* but it didn't say so. It was a general release.

'Damn!' she blazed. 'Oh, damn him!'

Without stopping to think she crumpled the pictures, shredded them, ripping them to pieces the same way Ben Standish had rent her heart in two. How could he have done this to her? How could he have wooed her, charmed her, loved her, and then turned around and taken photos that he would sell to some slick magazine for other men's thrills and his profit?

It was indecent, low and hateful. It was deceitful and it was wrong. Flinging the pillow to the floor, Jess stalked to the cupboard where he kept his photography equipment, yanked out the grey padded carry-all in which he stored his film, jerked open the velcro fasteners and spilled the contents on to the floor. There were more than a dozen rolls of already developed film. All the pictures he had taken on the expedition. And among them the nude photos of Jessica. And there was no way she was going to go through all of them looking for those that gave her pain.

Ben deserved a little pain, too.

Grabbing her backpack, she scooped up every roll of film and jammed them all inside. Then she bundled up her sleeping bag, tied it on to her pack and stood up, trembling, staring round at the havoc she had created.

Ben's camera lenses lay scattered on the floor. Unused rolls of film had rolled beneath the table. His sleeping bag lay in a heap in the driver's seat, and a confetti of glossy photographs littered every surface, torn, just as her dreams had been.

She took an angry swipe at her suddenly wet eyes. She hated her tears, hated caring enough to cry over Ben Standish. He didn't deserve it. He was as two-faced as he had ever been. She had just been too blind to see it.

Well, she was blind no longer. Kicking the door shut behind her, she shouldered her pack and walked out.

With luck she could hike to the nearest town and hitch a ride, getting miles away before he ever returned. And at this point, the more miles she put between Ben and herself, the better she would feel.

'SEE ANY WOLVES, THEN?' Geri Hamilton, the secretary, beamed at her when she walked into the NRRI office, the following morning. 'Besides Ben Standish, I mean.'

Jessica, who had been expecting just such a question, was able to school her features to reflect enthusiasm rather than the stark shaft of pain she felt at the mere sound of Ben's name. 'As a matter of fact, yes, I did.'

Geri's brows lifted. 'No kidding?'

It was just as well that she had, too, for being able to report on her wolf sightings gave them all something more substantial to talk about than how Jessica might have spent her weeks in the woods with Ben Standish.

Beyond a couple of teasing remarks from Geri and a disgruntled mumble from Matt, she escaped the preliminary queries unscathed.

She even decided that she dared say, 'I'm not really sure Ben will even do an article.'

'Why not?' demanded Gunnar, hating the thought that publicity he thought was certain might yet slip from his grasp. 'If you found wolves it should be a natural.'

Jess shrugged, unwilling to say much. The fewer untruths she told, the better. 'He didn't get any pictures of them. We saw them after dark.'

'He must have got pictures of something,' Matt said, giving her a speculative look. 'I mean, with *his* reputation...'

A dark tide of red coloured Jessica's cheeks and she ducked her head. Matt would have crowed long and loud if he had seen the pictures Ben had got! She clenched her teeth and counted to ten.

'I think he may have decided that I'm not much of a camera subject,' she lied, then thrust her thick report into Gunnar's hand to distract them. 'Here are the preliminary data. You might want to take a look before I leave today. If you have any questions we can discuss it before I leave on vacation.'

'When are you going?' Geri wanted to know.

'Tomorrow.'

If putting as many miles as possible between herself and Ben Standish had seemed a good idea yesterday, complete disappearance seemed the better part of valour today. Chances were, she told herself, he wouldn't bother confronting her for destroying his film. What he had done was far worse. Anyway, he probably wasn't obligated to *Preservation* for that particular article. And if he needed money, he could always find other naked ladies to photograph, she thought bitterly. Willing ones, this time.

But, just in case he decided to get testy about things, taking her already postponed vacation seemed like a good thing. And Gunnar, pleased with the results of her survey, had been only too happy to agree.

'Where are you going?' he asked.

'Hawaii.' Why not? she had thought. It seemed as good a choice as any. And maybe things there would remind her that men were not to be trusted. Not Kyle, not Ben. Not anyone as far as she could tell.

The day seemed to drag on for ever. And even when work ended and she knew she had to go home and pack for her vacation, Jessica couldn't summon much enthusiasm. She was aching, miserable, and still angry. Also exhausted enough to fall straight into bed. But she wouldn't sleep if she did, and she knew it. She hadn't slept the night before. All night she had tossed and turned, twisted by the cruel knowledge of his betrayal. She felt beaten, ravaged, tossed up on the shore like a broken bit of flotsam. Anger and depression swamped her in wave after wave.

The only thing to do, she decided, was to get on with the everyday tasks of life. It had been St Helena's humdrum routine that had saved her from Ben's perfidy the last time. Perhaps eating supper and paying the bills would do it now.

So she popped a frozen pizza into the oven, stuck a small bottle of wine into the fridge to chill, and began tearing up lettuce for salad. She tried to think about Hawaii, about the beach and sun and surf. But her mind had ideas of its own. One idea actually— Ben.

It was almost a relief, then, to hear the phone ring—until she picked it up.

'It's Kyle,' the strong, masculine voice said.

'I don't want—'

'Don't hang up, Jess,' he said quickly. 'Please!'

'Kyle, really, we've said all we—'

'I haven't. Lord, Jess, I've missed you! I've been calling every night.'

'I thought you'd get back together with your wife,' she said lamely, grasping at the straws.

There was a moment's confused silence. Then, 'Whatever made you think that?'

'Well, I mean, I just assumed that if I left . . .'

'No way,' said Kyle, adamant. 'We're through—honestly. I want you. Only you. I—'

'Kyle, no!'

'Oh, hell,' he muttered. 'This is useless. I'm coming over.'

'No,' she said again, but the phone went dead in her ear.

She was of half a mind not to answer the door when he arrived. She didn't want any more to do with him, no matter what he said. So what if she'd been wrong about Kyle and Tracey? That was the least of the things she'd been wrong about! But she didn't want to see him, regardless. And if she could have been certain he wouldn't make a scene on the porch, infuriating Mrs Franco, she would just have shouted at him to go away. After all, they had nothing left to say to each other. He was another one who hadn't changed. Apparently no man did—not Kyle, not Ben.

And damn it all, there she was, thinking about Ben again!

Jessica whacked the knife clear through the ripe tomato, squirting juice against the wall. Supper was supposed to be a calm, civilised meal. And it would have been, too, if she hadn't one ear cocked the whole time listening for Kyle's step on the stairs.

She knew at once she wasn't going to get away with not opening the door, not if she didn't want Mrs Franco to get an earful.

His steps were heavy, but the loud thundering of his fist literally made her drop her fork.

Be firm, she told herself. Be matter-of-fact. Be—

But her next words of self-help were drowned out in a loud, firm voice. 'You know I don't want to see you.'

'I'll damn well bet you don't!' a furious shout came back at her, and the pounding was renewed once more.

Ben!

She felt sudden terror. 'Go away!'

'Not on your life! Open the damn door!'

'Ben—'

'Open the door!'

It didn't take much imagination to guess what Mrs Franco must be thinking right now. Ben's fist hammered the door again.

Damn him! All right, if that was what he wanted, she would. Taking a deep breath, allowing it to fan the flames of her own well justified anger, Jessica flung open the door.

Ben pushed past her and walked into the room. There was nothing wolf-like about him now. He looked like a grizzly about to attack. On the far side of the room, he spun around, hooked his thumbs in his belt loops and glared at her. 'Where's my film?'

Jessica shut the door quietly and deliberately. 'Film?' she queried.

'My film, Jessica. Where is it?'

She gave him a small, self-satisfied smile. 'I threw it out.'

'You did *what?*'

He looked around for a waste basket, eyes searching frantically before coming back to rest once more on her. 'Where, Jessica?'

She shrugged lightly. 'In a Dumpster at the airport in Iron Mountain, Michigan.'

'*What?*'

Jessica didn't bother to repeat it. She knew he had heard her well enough the first time.

'Jeez!' Ben raked a furious hand through his hair. 'Why in heaven's name would you do something like that?'

Jessica's own fury kindled into full-blown flames then. 'Think about it,' she said, barely containing her anger. 'Maybe if you think *very* hard—'

He stopped cold next to the window that overlooked the lake. 'The photos?' he said quietly. 'The nude photos?'

Did he doubt it? 'Right in one.'

'Damn it, Jessica!' He stared at her incredulously, as if she were the one in the wrong, not him. 'Those were beautiful! Magnificent! They were—'

'They were taken without my permission, without my knowledge even.'

'So? It isn't as if I were going to—' Ben shook his head in disbelief. 'Wait a minute. You don't actually think I was going to sell those pictures, do you?'

Jessica met his outraged disbelief with stony silence.

'Jess, for goodness' sake!' he started to protest. 'I would never—'

'And, of course, you never have, have you, Ben?' she asked in syrupy tones.

'That was business!'

'Was it? Were those pictures of Clarissa a business proposition?' she asked bitterly.

Ben was silent. His fists clenched and he seemed to have stopped breathing. He looked white and anguished. 'Hell,' he muttered, and stalked to the window, staring out at the lake.

'I admit mine weren't quite as provocative as the ones you took of her, although they exposed me more.' Jess went on, still furious, 'But then you didn't have quite the same raw material to work with, did you? Nor did you have the co-operation!'

She clamped her jaws shut then, aware that her voice wavered and trembled. She wrapped her arms tightly against her chest, praying that she would not break down in front of him. It would be the ultimate humiliation, showing him how much she had trusted him, how truly she felt he had betrayed her.

'Forget the pictures of Clarissa,' said Ben heavily. He turned around and leaned his palms against the back of the sofa as he stood behind it. 'They had nothing to do with you.'

Jessica was saved from having to respond to that blatantly false remark by a tentative knock on the front door.

Oh heavens—Kyle! She had totally forgotten him. A few minutes ago she had dreaded the thought of his arrival. Now she was willing to welcome him with open arms. Perhaps he could get rid of Ben.

She opened the door at once, even managing to paste a half smile on her face.

'Kyle,' she began. 'Won't you co—'

'Who the hell are you?' demanded Ben, looming over her shoulder and breathing fire down her neck.

Kyle, who had been about to walk across the threshold, stayed right where he was.

He was taller than Ben, but his instincts of self-preservation were clearly better developed than those

of gallantry, for he blanched and said quickly, 'I'm—
er—Kyle Walters. And—er—you?' He offered his
hand tentatively.

Ben ignored it. 'Ben Standish. What do you
want?'

Kyle looked as if he had momentarily forgotten.
Then, clearing his throat he said, 'I was just coming
by to—er—visit with Jessica. She just got back
from—'

'I know where she was. I was with her,' Ben said
bluntly. Then, as if his pronouncement weren't clear
enough, he added, 'And she's leaving again. Now.
She doesn't have time to talk.'

Kyle looked from Ben to Jessica and back again,
obviously confused. 'Jess?' he asked at last, expecting her to resolve his questions.

If she had hoped he would scare Ben off, she had
misplaced her hopes. About all she could hope for
now, she decided, was that Ben's presence would get
rid of Kyle. It wasn't much, Ben being far the worse
prospect of the two, but it was all she had.

'You heard the man, Kyle,' she said finally, but
firmly.

Out of the corner of her eyes she saw Mrs Franco's curtains twitch.

'Goodbye,' Ben told him pointedly.

Jessica stared at Kyle mutely, half torn between
entreaty and despair. Just go, she wanted to say. Ben

had never struck her as particularly civilised. And things were bad enough without the possibility of bloodshed on her porch.

Kyle shifted from one foot to the other, assessing Ben's claim to her and obviously coming to the same conclusion. He shrugged. 'Well then, goodbye,' he said.

He had scarcely turned around before Ben shut the door behind him.

'Now then, where were we?' he demanded. He was still looking over her, and his nearness made her edgy.

'You were just leaving.'

'No.' He smiled, a decidedly grim smile. 'I think we have a few things to get settled first.'

'I don't want to talk to you any more than I wanted to talk to him.'

'Don't talk, then,' Ben said abruptly. 'Listen.'

He stalked over to the overstuffed chair next to the fireplace and sat down in it. Short of grabbing him by the arm and trying to haul him back out of it, Jess didn't see any alternative to listening. Not that he could say anything that would make her forgive him this time.

She leaned back against the small bar that separated the living-room from the kitchen and regarded him with what she hoped was cool indifference. Inside she was having to bank the flames of an anger that still threatened to burn out of control.

The object now was simply to endure him, to steel herself to hear whatever garbage he offered as an explanation, and then to see him on his way out of her life. Permanently.

'So talk,' she said ungraciously.

'I didn't take those photos of your mother.'

'You—'

'Just shut up and listen, damn it!' He half rose from his chair, his body tautly coiled, like a cat about to spring.

Jessica subsided against the bar, sceptical, but waiting.

'Clarissa was afraid she was over the hill, afraid she wouldn't get any more juicy parts after *Passion's Game.* She wanted some publicity.'

'She had a publicity man.'

Ben rubbed a hand round the back of his neck, clearly uncomfortable. 'Not that kind of publicity,' he said. He didn't look at her. His eyes drilled holes in her carpet.

'Oh?'

He sighed. 'She wanted to be thought of as young, attractive, desirable...'

'She wanted you. And she got you.'

'No.'

'Oh, come on, Ben. I waited and waited for you that day. Remember? Little dumb Jessica sat out on the point and thought you were going to come to her when all the time you were going away with her mother!'

'It wasn't like that!'

Jessica snorted inelegantly.

Ben's jaw tightened and he slammed his fist against his thigh. 'Damn it, Jessica!'

She put her hand over her mouth, though whether it was a sob or a laugh she was smothering she didn't know. 'Sorry,' she said composedly after a moment. 'Do go on with your fascinating tale.'

He stared hard at her. 'I never took those photos, and I never made love to your mother.'

'Just had sex with her, did you?'

'No!' He jumped up and paced across the living-room. 'I have never, I repeat, *never,* known your mother in the intimate sense of the word.'

Jess rolled her eyes. 'So did I imagine it all?' she asked sarcastically. 'That wasn't you she left with? It wasn't you she showed up at parties with? Got written up in gossip mags with?'

Ben drew a long, unsteady breath. 'It wasn't the way you think.'

She arched a sceptical brow. 'Oh? And pray tell, what do I think?'

Ben scowled and jammed his fists in the pockets of his jeans. 'You think I stole her away from your father, followed her around like some sex-crazed gigolo, took her picture and exploited it for all it was worth, then rode off into the sunset unscathed!'

'And I'm wrong?'

'Yes.'

'Convince me.'

'Heck.' He rubbed his hand around the back of his collar again, ruffling the thick dark hair that brushed the nape of his neck. Then he sighed and sat back down on the edge of the chair he had vacated just moments before. Resting his elbows on his knees, he steepled his fingers in front of his mouth.

'You remember how things were eight years ago?' he asked finally.

Only too well, Jessica thought. She nodded briefly, perfunctorily, hoping that he wouldn't do a postmortem. She had done enough of her own.

'Between us?' Ben pressed.

Colour rose unbidden in her cheeks. 'We're not talking about us!'

'I am.' Ben's voice was flat. 'I was attracted to you. I wanted to go to bed with you. And you were only sixteen years old, for heaven's sake!'

'That's not my fault!' Jess raged.

'Of course not! But it was bloody difficult keeping my hands off you, and you know it! I almost didn't manage it!'

'So?' she asked belligerently.

'So you and I weren't the only ones who knew it.'

'What do you mean by that?'

'Clarissa knew it, too.'

'She never said a word to me!'

'Did you two talk about that sort of thing?'

'Well, not really, but—'

'Believe me, she knew,' he assured her.

'Well, what if she did?' Jess said defensively, recalling now a few of Clarissa's hard looks and biting remarks about the way Jess chased Ben.

'She didn't like it. Not one little bit.' Ben's voice was bitter. 'Although I really can't say I blame her.'

'But what does that have to do with anything?'

'It has to do with why I left with her,' he said. He laced his fingers, the knuckles white. 'I started going around with her in the first place just so I would be able to keep my hands off you. And then when I did, Clarissa discovered that being in the company of a "younger man"—' he gave Jess a sardonic look '—caused people to take another look at her. She liked it. A lot. She wasn't getting any younger. She could see that every time she looked at you. And being with me was good for her career.'

Jess stared at him. 'Not a little conceited, are you?'

'I'm telling you the truth, Jessica. She was going to leave Max anyway. She just needed a man to do it with.'

'And of course, you offered?' She spoke with saccharine sweetness, wondering how deep a hole he would dig himself into.

'She said she'd tell Max I made love to you if I didn't.'

Jessica's mouth dropped open. He had hit rock bottom with that.

Ben met her stare unflinching. His fingers tightened.

For what seemed like aeons neither spoke. What, after all, she wondered, was there to say?

Of all the preposterous excuses she might have imagined that he would come up with, that was the most implausible thing she had ever heard. She shut her eyes in the vain hope that when she opened them she would find that the whole ghastly mess was nothing more than a dream.

But it wasn't. When she opened them, he was still there, his hazel eyes meeting her own.

'That's absurd,' she said at last.

'It's true.' Ben ran a hand through his hair. 'You know that the one person Max really cared about was you. You were his chip off the old block.' He sighed. 'Look at it from my side, for heaven's sake. If Clarissa had told him that I had made love to you, he wouldn't have given me the benefit of the doubt. He could see what was going on between us!'

'*Nothing* was going on between us!' Jessica shouted. 'Nothing happened between us at all!'

'We were tinder ready to explode and you know it. Max knew it. So did Clarissa,' he added roughly. 'And if she had fed Max's worries about his darling daughter, you can jolly well bet my career would have gone up in smoke.'

'Ah!'

'What do you mean, "*ah*"?' he demanded.

'I mean, I am beginning to get a faint glimpse of understanding,' Jess said sarcastically. 'How very fortunate for you! You could use Mother and get away from me both at the same time, furthering your career as well.'

Ben said a very rude word and stalked across the living-room again, slamming his fist against the wall. 'You have the most incredible facility for misunderstanding everything I say!'

'On the contrary, I think I'm making perfect sense,' she contradicted him. 'The only misunderstanding I did was when we were at White Birch Bay. There I thought you might have changed. I can see how very wrong I was. I suppose in a way I ought to be grateful you took those pictures. Now I know. Some things never change.'

'You don't,' Ben said sharply. 'You're just as pig-headed now as you were when we started this trip. You don't listen at all! I told you, I didn't take those pictures of your mother!'

'It was just a nasty rumour?' Jess asked sarcastically.

'Something like that.' He didn't say anything else and Jessica wondered whether he expected her to take him at his word, even after all this.

He paced around the living-room as if debating what to say. Whatever it was, it couldn't be more unlikely than everything else he had told her tonight. She frowned at him. 'Well?' she prodded.

'You know the guy we saw at Mackinac?'

'Neil?'

'No, the other one. When we left. Torberg, the guy on the dock.'

'Yes.' One of the most distasteful men she had ever seen.

'You remember I said he was a photographer?'

'Oh, come on...' Jess began. 'Surely you don't expect me to believe...'

'Unlikely as it may seem,' Ben said harshly, 'he's got talent. He has a certain type of vision. He—'

'He certainly does,' said Jess drily. 'But you can't make me believe my mother would let him...let him...'

Ben gazed at her, not saying anything, but she knew that was exactly what he was trying to make her believe. When she finally stammered to a complete halt, he rested his chin on his fist and said softly, 'She did, Jess.'

'But the magazine said, "CLARISSA EVANS— THE WOMAN ONLY HER LOVER KNOWS!"' she quoted, the headline of the article emblazoned on her memory even after all these years. 'Her lover,' she repeated slowly and with emphasis.

'Her lover, yes. Not me.'

'Torberg?' Jessica was incredulous. 'But—but—but she was *beautiful,* and he's—he's—' she faltered, unable to adequately describe the man she had seen on the dock.

'He's talented,' Ben told her. 'And Clarissa knew it. It suited her to let people think I took them, though. I had better press appeal than Walt,' he added wryly. 'People thought I was her lover. And...' he shrugged, 'I guess at the time I couldn't see how letting the rumour go would hurt anything. And Walt is a bit of a creep. It did wonders for my career,' he added wryly. 'You'd be amazed how many women wanted me to photograph them after that.'

'So you were saving her reputation?' she demanded.

'I guess you could say that.'

Jess couldn't even reply. The things he told her were too hard to believe. She had spent the last eight years believing he had taken those pictures. Heaven knew, the whole world thought he had taken those pictures. Why now was she supposed to believe he had not? Except because it suited him.

Her jaw tightened and she stared at him, angry again, certain that once more he had almost played her for a fool. 'I don't believe you,' she told him flatly. 'I don't believe a word of it! Not a word.'

Ben looked at her long and hard, as if he were probing her defences for signs of weakness. But Jess didn't have any. Not now. She had let him persuade her for the last time.

He seemed to realise that, for finally he nodded his head briefly, acknowledging her stony stare. Then he rocked on his heels and said, 'Don't, then. But whether you do or not, you owe me some pictures.'

His whole tone of voice changed as he spoke. Gone was the desperate note she had just heard in his explanations. Gone was the pleading. And in its place she heard the sound of steel, hard and cold.

'I need all the rest of my pictures, Jessica.'

Jess stared at him, her face mutinous. 'Too bad. Guess you're out of luck. Sorry about that.'

She wasn't, and both of them knew it. No matter what else happened she would never be sorry about that. He deserved it.

'They're gone?' he pressed. 'You're certain?'

'Absolutely certain.'

'You owe me, then,' he said, his tone ominous.

'Like hell!'

'You destroyed two weeks of my work.'

You damned near destroyed me! Jess wanted to shout at him. But she gave an uncaring little shrug. 'So don't do the article. You won't starve.'

'It was commissioned, Jessica. I was given an advance.'

'Give it back.'

'I can't. I don't have the money. I put it down on my property in Missouri.'

'Sure you did,' she said, disbelieving even that. A penthouse, more likely. In Manhattan.

'I did,' Ben said implacably. 'And even if I hadn't, I wouldn't give it back now. I'm doing the article. It's a matter of principle.'

'Fancy you talking about principles!' Jess gave him a scornful, bitter look. 'Take out a loan,' she suggested.

'No. I'm doing the article. *We're* doing the article, I should say,' he told her, a grim smile creasing his face.

'No.'

'Oh yes. Yes, we are. You can just pack your backpack all over again, sweetheart, because we're going back there now.'

'I'm not,' Jessica said stoutly, backing away from him as he advanced on her.

'You are.'

'I'm on holiday as of tomorrow. I'm going to Hawaii.'

He shook his head. 'No, you're not. You're coming with me—tonight.'

'I can't.'

'You can. And you will.'

'No.'

'I wonder what the highly esteemed Mr Halversen would have to say about that,' Ben speculated. 'He seems to like publicity. The right sort anyway,' he added, a cruel smile playing about his mouth. His voice was smooth now, his eyes piercing.

'You wouldn't write—'

He smiled sardonically. 'Wouldn't I just?'

He would, and Jessica knew it.

'But—'

'No buts, Jessica. Tonight. If you've unpacked, tough. You'll just have to pack again. Don't worry, I'll wait.'

So saying, he turned and dropped into the chair by the fireplace where he had sat earlier. But this time he didn't look earnest or imploring at all. He looked hard and implacable. He leaned back and crossed one leg over the other, resting his ankle on the other knee, then locked his arms behind his head.

'Take your time if you want, Jessica,' he said. 'But we're going back tonight and we're going to reshoot the pictures for my article, and I don't give a damn if you like it or not.'

CHAPTER NINE

ALOHA, HAWAII, Jessica thought bitterly as she averted her eyes from a pair of oncoming headlights. Well, she hadn't really been dying to go there anyway.

But that was about as much optimism towards her present predicament as she could muster, because she wasn't dying to go back to White Birch Bay either. Especially not in the company of Ben Standish.

She had been right about his civilised veneer—it didn't run deep. A few more comments about what Gunnar's reaction to her little temper tantrum would be, added to what he told her he would say about her professional competence and demeanour, as well as the way he drummed his fingers impatiently on his thigh while he sat in the chair glaring at her, and she had repacked her backpack.

'I'll do it,' she told him coldly, 'but I won't like it.'

'You won't be the only one,' he assured her. It was the last thing he said to her until he stopped the truck just outside Menominee, Michigan, an hour before.

'What are you stopping for?' Jessica had demanded.

'I'm bushed,' he told her. 'I drove all last night. Your turn.'

She considered that, weighing her options.

'Don't even think it,' he said, his voice ominous. 'If I wake up and find you've turned around, there'll be hell to pay, sweetheart. You can count on it.'

Jess knew she could. 'Yes, sir,' she said sarcastically, moving into the seat he had vacated. 'Anything else, sir?'

But Ben didn't reply. He just made his way to the back of the camper and flung himself down on the bunk. He was asleep even before she got the truck started again.

Jessica glanced over her shoulder at the unmoving dark shape curled on the bunk. Rat, she called him silently. Dismal, rotten rat. How could he have stood there in her apartment and lied to her like that? How could he tell her that he had had no intention of selling those photos? How could he have denied taking the pictures of her mother? Or having been her mother's lover?

Her fingers strangled the steering wheel. She despised him, hated him. And—she blinked back her tears and gave a fierce sniff—she hated the way she had learned to care about him, to love him again!

She gritted her teeth noisily, but Ben slept on, oblivious.

He snored like a pig, she thought, and she purposefully took the next curve too sharply, hoping with childish malice to knock him right off the bunk. Unfortunately he slept on, undisturbed.

Not until she had driven another hour and a half did he awake. Without warning he slipped into the passenger seat alongside her, rubbing his eyes and saying, 'I'll drive now.'

'Fine with me,' Jess said shortly. She pulled over on to the shoulder and cut the ignition. 'Be my guest.' She stood up, averting her eyes from his tousled dark hair, stubbled cheeks and sleepy eyes. Too many memories stabbed her, reminding her of other times during the past couple of weeks when she had seen him that way—not quite awake, a little muzzy and cuddly-looking. She had loved making love with him then. The loving had started slowly, with gentle touches, soft kisses and— Damn it, what was she thinking about that for!

'Thank you for driving,' he said as he eased the camper back on to the narrow highway.

'Don't expect me to say you're welcome.' She got to her feet and moved to the back of the camper, needing to get away from him. Her body hadn't yet assimilated her mind's feelings. It foolishly still wanted him.

'I don't expect anything from you, Jessica,' he said in a grating voice, 'except for the minimum of co-operation expected of any professional.'

And that, Jessica was determined to see, would be exactly what he got. No more. No less.

It was the hardest assignment she had ever had in her life.

Ben set up their camp slowly and deliberately, making Jessica do the same. They ran through every basic camping technique what seemed like countless times to Jess, while he fiddled with apertures and lenses and told her to move this way or that.

'You didn't make this big a fuss last time,' she snarled at him.

He smiled and kept on fiddling with the camera. 'Move over. You're in the shadows.'

Gritting her teeth, she complied. The weather was hotter than the last time they had come, muggier. The insects seemed fiercer too. Everything was conspiring against them as far as Jessica could see. She seethed inwardly, hating Ben even more for his apparently cool unflappability.

'Take off your hat. I can't see your face,' he said.

Her temper got the better of her then. 'You've taken enough pictures. My word, you must have taken all of these a million times before!'

Ben smiled sardonically. 'How true. I wonder whatever happened to that first batch. They seem to have vanished. Haven't they, Jessica?'

'That was your fault!'

Ben just looked at her in wordless disgust.

She clenched her fists and wondered how much longer he was going to persist in putting her through this farce. 'Just get on with it, then!'

Ben did. Over the next three days he put her through the hoops as far as Jessica was concerned. He took pictures of her cooking over the open campfire, stalking a raccoon through the woods, washing out her shirt in the lake, and a thousand other stupid things she was sure he thought of just to annoy her.

'Isn't there anything else you'd like a picture of?' she snapped at him finally one hot, steamy afternoon, while it threatened to storm.

Ben's eyes gleamed ferally. 'Now that you mention it...' he drawled.

Jessica bristled.

He laughed. 'Just kneel by the creek bed then, pretend you've found some wolf tracks.' And he waited, a mocking smile still curling the corner of his mouth while she complied, trying to disguise her fury.

Her shirt was sticking to her back, perspiration was running down between her breasts. She itched as if a thousand mosquitoes were chewing her. All she wanted was a dip in the lake. And there was no way she was going to get one. Not with Ben Standish within five miles of here!

'Look interested, damn it!' Ben snarled, squatting down to get a closer shot of her. 'This is your career, for heaven's sake!'

Jessica tried to look interested.

'Relax!' Ben demanded.

Then, five seconds later, 'Look serious, for crying out loud!'

'Brush the hair out of your eyes!'

'Stop looking like you're made of stone, Jessica!'

And Jessica, tired of trying, gave up. 'I'm not a bloody photographer's model!' she flared at him, standing up and flinging a handful of mud into his face. 'You take me the way you see me, and that's it!'

'I took you the way I saw you,' he told her cruelly, 'and you didn't like it one bit!'

'You're damned right I didn't! It was a low, rotten, sneaky thing to do. The sort of typical behaviour I would expect from a bas—'

'That's enough!'

'Don't tell me when something is enough, Ben Standish!'

'Be quiet, Jessica,' Ben ordered with cold fury. 'You're beginning to sound just like your mother!'

'Isn't that what you wanted?' Jess's voice was shrill, all effort to control her anger gone now, her temper like a lid on a pot now blown sky high. 'A little sweet talk, a little roll in the grass, a few clicks of the camera and *voilà*—'

Ben grabbed the front of her shirt and hauled her against his chest so she could feel as well as hear his anger. 'I said, that's enough! I always thought you were ten thousand times the woman your mother was! I thought you were heaven on earth! I guess I was wrong! You don't know any more about love than she did!'

And with that, he let go of her, spun away and strode off down the creek, his back stiff with fury.

Jessica stood, shaken and trembling in his wake. 'I hate you,' she muttered, blinking back hot tears. 'I hate you!'

And she turned and ran off into the woods, not caring how far she went or in what direction as long as it took her far, far away from Ben.

How dared he say that about her? She *was* ten thousands times the woman her mother was—in every way that truly mattered. She might not have Clarissa's sexy reputation, but she had more compassion, more caring, more *love*—regardless of what Ben Standish thought!

She bit her lip angrily, coming to a stop near the wolves' clearing. Far off she could hear the faint rumble of thunder. An echo of her own emotions. She sank down on to a log, weary, angry, too upset to do anything but sit and gasp for breath.

The thunder moved closer. It wouldn't be long until the rain began. She wiped a sweaty hand across her smudged, dirty face, thinking that she would welcome it. She needed something to cool her rampaging emotions as well as her grimy body. Through the trees she could see the sky darkening overhead, pewter and brass mixing as the wind began to move the clouds across the sky above her.

A shaft of lightning sizzled in the distance, and Jess tipped her face up to receive the first spatters of rain.

It began coming down in earnest, filtering through the trees, big spats dropping on to her head, cooling her off as they made rivulets in the dust on her face. And she breathed easier, forgetting briefly her anger with Ben. She moved out into the clearing, knowing the wolves wouldn't be around because she hadn't seen them since she and Ben had come back.

The rain sluiced down, drenching her. The thunder rumbled even closer. Suddenly she heard Ben's voice calling her name. Without thinking she darted back into the trees. She wasn't ready to see him yet. She was still mad. The last thing she needed was more of his obnoxious protectiveness, his overbearing attitude. He was the one who hated storms, not her! Why didn't he just go back to the tents without her?

She saw him move through the trees quite a distance away, heard him call her name again over the sound of the approaching thunder. 'Go away,' she muttered, and made her way stealthily through the trees beyond the clearing even deeper into the forest.

The lightning jagged around her, the thunder shook the ground beneath her feet. She knew Ben would be hating it and felt a pang of guilt that he was out in it because of her. But then, she thought, she knew how to take care of herself. He didn't have to be. Not for her sake!

She found shelter against some large boulders, huddling down, grateful to be out of the rain now that it was pelting down. She was frankly surprised that Ben had bothered to come looking for her. Why had he bothered? There was no love lost between them—not any more.

When the worst of the storm had passed, Jessica picked her way back through the forest. She felt lucky to have encountered shelter where she had. Two trees were charred and blackened, both still smouldered. One was split clear through. The other had lost its largest branch. Jessica shuddered as she passed it. Perhaps there was something to this aversion of Ben's after all.

Suddenly she felt an overpowering need to go home—to get away from the violence of nature and of man. Ben had enough pictures. And she had had more than enough of him. No matter how much she would have liked to bear up indifferently under his demands, she couldn't take this emotional battering any longer. She needed to get away from him once and for all. She needed to go home.

She came out of the woods about a hundred yards east of their campsite, and stood for a moment on the dunes watching the wind whip frothy waves against the shore. To the west the sky was still dark, as if nature had decided one storm wasn't enough, and was all set to provide another.

The campsite appeared deserted. Jessica smiled smugly as she walked towards it. Probably Ben was still in his tent with his head under his knapsack.

Well, it didn't matter, she told herself. She didn't want to see him anyway.

For a moment the sun broke through, bathing the beach and the lake in a burnished golden glow. Then, just as quickly it was gone, and Jessica heard thunder again. She scowled and headed up the beach towards the tents.

'Ben?' she called, almost reluctantly, just to reassure herself that he had got back.

There was no answer.

'Ben!'

Nothing.

She strode over to his tent. 'Ben, are you in there?'

She waited for a moment, then jerked the zipper up, knowing she would feel like a complete fool if he was sitting there smirking at her. But she wasn't entirely relieved either to find that he was not. His camera was there, but Ben was gone.

So where was he?

The wind was picking up again, moving slate-coloured clouds rapidly across the sky. Jess stared into the empty tent, hands on her hips, wondering just what sort of nonsense he was trying to pull now.

She glanced all around, half expecting to see him standing by a tree, laughing at her. But she didn't see him anywhere.

Perhaps he had gone too far into the forest looking for her and had holed up somewhere until it wasn't raining so hard. Yes, she decided, that must be it. Well, he had better hurry or he was going to catch it again. Already she could see more lightning off to the west zigzagging across the sky.

She went back into her own tent and changed out of her wet, grimy clothes, putting on a pair of dry jeans and a plaid shirt. Then, topping that with a bright green rain slicker, she clambered back out and looked around again.

'Ben?' she shouted. 'Hey, you can come out now, Ben!'

But he didn't answer.

The rain began and, starting to worry a bit, Jessica retreated to her tent. If this was a joke, some perverse bit of nastiness he had cooked up just to get her to show that she cared about him still, it was sick.

Thunder rocked the earth beneath her feet and a sharp burst of lightning split the sky. If it was a joke, she decided, then it was definitely a joke on Ben.

This storm was, if anything, worse than the first. And by the time it had expended its fury on the beach where Jessica huddled in her tent, she was well and truly concerned. *Where in heaven's name was Ben?*

She crept back out of her tent and surveyed the damage. Ben's tent was tilting, battered by the heavy winds and shifting sands. Her own was little better. The laundry she had hung out that morning was flung about, draped over bushes, lying in muddy heaps on the ground. But Jessica scarcely paid any attention. Her whole mind was otherwise occupied. She wanted to find Ben.

A noise behind her caused her to spin around. But it was only a raccoon that skittered down from a tree and ambled off towards the creek. As she stood there she began to hear subtle movements and see evidence of other animals leaving their hiding places.

But of Ben there was no sign.

She followed the raccoon to the creek. Swollen, tea-coloured water hurtled and burbled towards the lakeshore, almost surging above the banks as it went.

Damn it, where was Ben?

It was still raining as she worked her way inland, keeping close to the stream, calling his name. The water soaked her jeans, and sluiced down her neck beneath the slicker, leaving her shirt cold and clammy against her skin.

Already dusk, it was getting hard to see. She wondered if she had missed him. Or was he just not answering as she hadn't answered him earlier?

'Answer me, damn you!' she shouted, turning on the flashlight she had brought with her now. But she didn't hear anything save the night noises that were normal in the forest. They didn't bother her at all. She had no fear of noises or sights or things that went bump in the night. Her only fear was the very specific, growing fear she felt for Ben's safety.

And when at last her flashlight arced across the creek and lit up his still, prone form pinned beneath the limbs of a lightning-splintered tree, her fear changed rapidly to the panic she had been trying to keep at bay for so long.

'Ben!'

He was facedown in the mud, silent and unmoving.

Heedless of the churning water, Jessica plunged across the creek, scrabbling for a hold on the slick, smooth rocks, impervious to the icy water spilling inside her hiking boots. Reaching him at last, she dropped to her knees and shined the flashlight directly on his face. His eyes were shut, his lips slightly parted. She dropped the light to the ground and ran her fingers over his back, thanking God for the shallow rise and fall of his breathing.

'Ben?' Her voice was urgent, frantic.

A heavy limb pinned his legs, half-burying them in mud. A smaller one had nailed his left arm to the ground. But most worrying of all was the stone she found flush against his temple and the bruised lump that welled where it had hit.

She scrambled to her feet and tried to drag the tree limbs off him. Grabbing the one that had clipped his shoulder, she bent it back, pulling with all her strength. She gritted her teeth, braced her boots as best she could in the mud, and tugged and tugged.

'Come on,' she urged. 'Come on, you bloody great tree! Move!'

And with a sudden crack, the limb snapped.

Jess went flat on her rear end in the mud. 'Thank God!' She scrambled to her feet, rejoicing in a moment's victory.

But it was short-lived. No matter how hard she pulled, the larger limb would not budge. It held him

fast. And, even as she tried, rivulets of rain mingled
with tears of despair and desperation on her cheeks.

'Hell,' she moaned. 'Oh, hell. Oh, Ben!'

Then she bent to pick up the flashlight and shone
it again in Ben's face. He groaned and tried to turn
his head.

Jess dropped at once to his side. 'Ben? Can you
hear me?'

'J-Jess?' He got a mouthful of mud for his effort,
and Jessica clawed away at the area surrounding his
face.

'It's all right.' She touched his cheek, reassuring.
'Don't worry, it'll be all right. I'll get help.'

'You . . . all right?' he muttered. 'Die . . . people
die . . . lightning.'

'You won't die, Ben!' Her tears were choking her.
'You won't! I won't let you!'

But he seemed to be slipping away right before her
eyes. She shone the light on his face again.

'Ben, listen to me,' she implored. 'I can't move the
tree limb that's pinning you down. I've got to get
help. I'll be back as quick as I can.'

She thought he nodded. She hoped he nodded. She
had no other choice. Unthinking, she bent and kissed
his cold cheek. 'I'll take care of everything,' she
promised, and prayed that it was true.

Never in her life had Jessica run so hard and so
fast for so long. She battled her way through the

woods, then ran heavily along the wave-dashed shoreline, cursing her heavy boots all the way. But when she had to slough through the underbrush to where they had left the camper, she was grateful for them. Still, she thought her heart would burst, and the painful stitch in her side threatened to rend her in half. But still she ran.

Barely stopping to wipe her hands and face on a dirty engine rag, she flung herself into the driver's seat of the camper and started the engine.

'Come on, come on!' she urged as it sputtered reluctantly to life.

It seemed, she thought later, as if those two words were all she said all night.

She drove quickly to the nearest town, got the bartender in the one open business in town to phone for the state police, and, with no cajoling at all, discovered that half the bar at least was willing to come back and help her get Ben dug out.

One man ran home for his chain saw. One went for blankets, and the bartender thrust a bottle of brandy in her hands as she ran out the door.

'You give him this,' he instructed her. 'It's good for what ails ya.' He looked her up and down, then added, 'You have a nip too, sweetheart.'

Jessica mumbled her thanks.

'Just go on now,' he told her. 'There's plenty of 'em will follow ya. I'll point the cops in the right direction.'

Eight men came with her or followed in an all-terrain vehicle. More shouted as they left that another truckload would be coming after. It was a bit of excitement, she decided. A bright spot of action in an otherwise humdrum day. But she couldn't blame them; she could only be grateful for their assistance.

And as she tore away in the camper, leaving a great spray of water and mud in her wake, she muttered once more, 'Come on. Come on!'

She did the same as she led them back through the woods.

'It's not far. Come on,' she urged them, sensing that more than a few were beginning to flag, even through the ATV had eliminated the several-mile run along the shore that she had done earlier. 'Please, come on. Hurry!'

Ben was unconscious when they finally returned. No amount of light shone in his eyes got any response at all, but Jessica wouldn't stop trying. It was her fault, she told herself. She had done this to him. And she knelt beside him, talking to him, exhorting him to wake up again, though the sound of the chain saws drowned out everything else in the air.

By the time the tree was cut away and removed, the police had arrived, bringing with them two Emergency Medical Technicians, still panting from their run through the woods.

They lifted Ben carefully on to the stretcher, then picked it up, and with Jessica walking silently alongside, they made their way carefully but steadily back downstream towards the shore.

The darkness kept her from seeing how really awful Ben looked. Probably, she decided later, it was a blessing. If she had seen then the deathly pallor of his face and the blueish tinge to his lips, she doubted if she would have mustered the courage to stumble to the beach.

As it was all she could see was the outline of his body wrapped loosely in blankets, and the darker profile of his face, his black hair plastered against his forehead by rain water and blood.

On the beach the ragged procession halted and all the townsmen stepped back respectfully while the EMTs slid the stretcher slowly into the ATV they had come in.

Without asking, Jessica scrambled in after him.

'What about your tents, miss?' one of the men asked.

'It's not important,' she said. Nothing was now, save Ben. But then she remembered his film and his cameras. She had to save them. Regardless of how things were between them, she knew she owed him that.

'Wait,' she told the policeman. 'I'll just be a minute.'

She grabbed the grey carry-all and the camera that lay on his sleeping bag, then, clutching them against her chest, she ran back to climb into the vehicle.

She heard the police radioing ahead to the hospital. The smells of alcohol and disinfectant blended with those of wet mud and exhaust as she slumped next to Ben's inert form.

'Miss?' One of the men from the bar held something out to her just as the door was about to close. It was the bottle of brandy.

Jessica's fingers wrapped around it numbly. 'Thank you,' she muttered. Not just for the brandy, but for everything.

CHAPTER TEN

IT'S ALL MY FAULT.

The words echoed endlessly in Jessica's mind as the rescue vehicle sped down the lonely narrow highway through the night. They echoed as the medical personnel at the tiny hospital whisked Ben away from her and into the glaring lights of the emergency room. And they continued to echo while she sat waiting—and waiting—on the hard, cold plastic chair in the corridor just outside the room.

It was all her fault.

If she just hadn't run off without answering him when he shouted for her... If she hadn't left the campsite angry in the first place... If she hadn't destroyed his film so they had had to return to White Birch Bay... There was no end to the *ifs* that plagued her. And no end to the waiting either.

She looked up hopefully every time a nurse or doctor hurried in or out, but no one even glanced at her. They only muttered about blood and concussion, internal injuries and complications. It was not reassuring.

Ben hadn't regained consciousness on the journey, and Jessica had had more than enough time to contemplate his bleak, ravaged features and feel a pain worse than any she could have imagined. Her anger with him—her sense of betrayal—which she had worn like a shield ever since she had found the pictures, slipped now and shattered into a million pieces. There was no way she could pretend that he didn't matter to her even now, and she felt bleak, hollow, cold and guilty. She knew that whatever Ben Standish might or might not have done, he didn't deserve this.

She watched the comings and goings of the doctors, her mind conjuring up all the worst possibilities. The longer they took the greater her fears grew until she began to wonder if he would even survive.

When at last one of the doctors did emerge and beckon to her, she could barely get to her feet she was trembling so. But he slipped an arm under her elbow, giving her support as he said matter-of-factly, 'Cracked ribs, broken collarbone, broken arm, multiple lacerations and bruises. We don't know the full extent of his head injuries yet.'

My God, Jessica wanted to say, isn't that enough? But she grasped at the hope that Ben would recover and nodded mutely, then asked, 'May I see him?'

'For a moment. We're waiting for the helicopter now. We'll be flying him to Petoskey as soon as we can.'

She gulped. 'To Petoskey?'

'They have excellent neurological facilities.'

She didn't know if that was good news or bad. She felt herself start trembling again.

The doctor gave her what she imagined was intended to be an encouraging smile, but which in fact looked positively sepulchral. She winced, then dropped her eyes and walked slowly into the emergency room to be with Ben.

He lay cold and still on the gurney beneath bright lights, his eyes closed and his lips slightly parted. Only the reassuringly steady rise and fall of his chest gave her any comfort at all.

Though he was covered with a stark white sheet, she could see the outline of the binding around his ribcage and the brace that held his collarbone in place. His broken arm had been placed in a plaster cast and lay across his stomach, supported by a pillow to keep it from resting against his ribs.

Jessica approached him warily, as if somehow he would sense her presence and open his eyes to glare at her accusingly. He had every right. Although if he did, she doubted if the pain she felt could be any worse than it was already.

She reached out and touched his cheek gently. It was cold and slightly rough with day-old beard. She trailed her fingers over it lightly, but Ben didn't respond.

'I'm sorry,' she told him in a broken whisper. 'I'm so sorry. I never meant for it to come to this.'

The tears she had been holding back now spilled over, rolling down her cheeks, dripping on to Ben's own cheeks where they lay glistening until she dabbed them carefully off.

'Why did you come after me?' she asked him, agonised.

Why indeed? It was a question that had nagged at her ever since the storm. At first she wouldn't let herself consider the reasons. They hinted that he actually cared about her, that she might have been wrong about him, about his motives, about the truth of all the things he had told her. But now?

Now she wasn't sure. Now her mind was in a muddle. She didn't know what to think, what to believe, what to do. Except to take care of Ben now. She owed him that much at least.

The helicopter arrived, and with a great deal of persuasive talking, Jessica got permission to accompany him to Petoskey.

'What if he wakes and wonders where he is? What if he asks what happened? Disorientation wouldn't be good for him,' she argued desperately. 'He'll need someone familiar.'

And eventually the doctors agreed.

'But he might not come around for a while,' one of them cautioned her.

He didn't. For days.

Jessica thought she would lose her mind. She got a tiny room in a motel not far from the hospital. But she was rarely there, preferring to spend all her time with a still comatose Ben. The only times she left him were when the nurses threw her out and when she took his film to the photography shop nearby to get it developed. She knew Ben would have preferred to do his own developing, but that was out of the question now. But she told the man in the shop whose photographs he was going to be doing, in hope that he would do a good job.

The man's eyes widened. '*The* Ben Standish? The one who did that fantastic layout of grizzlies in the *Geographic?*'

Jessica, who had been prepared to hear Ben praised for layouts he had done of a far different type, depending on whichever slick men's magazine this man read, looked at him as surprised as he had been a moment before. 'Yes,' she said, 'that's him.'

'He's the best there is. What's he doing here?'

She explained about the survey, about Ben's article.

'On the Upper Peninsula, you say?' The man frowned. 'Then why is he here?'

And she told him about the accident.

The next morning it was all over town.

The local newspaper sent a reporter to talk to Jessica, the radio services picked it up, and because it was a dull day everywhere apparently, so did the national news.

'We're famous!' one of the nurses giggled.

But Jessica scarcely noticed because something far more important happened at the same time—Ben opened his eyes.

For a moment she thought she was hallucinating. It was late evening, in the vague fuzzy sort of half-light that lingers in the north, and she had been sitting there intermittently dozing and staring at him for several hours, willing him to respond.

Suddenly, quite without warning, Ben's eyes opened and he blinked.

'Ben?' She was leaning over his bed in an instant.

His gaze wavered, his eyelids flickered, and he opened parched lips to make the faintest thread of sound.

Jessica grabbed one of the tiny sponges in the water glass beside his bed and touched it to his lips. 'There.' She smiled at him, tears welling. 'Better?'

Her heart hammered wildly. She knew, in some remote corner of her mind, that she ought to be racing down the hall fetching a nurse right now, but she didn't move an inch.

'Good,' he murmured, and his eyes tried to focus on her again. 'Jess.' And his lids shut once more and he sighed softly.

Jessica, weeping with joy, bent to kiss him, then ran for the nurse. 'He's awake!' she cried. 'He's all right. Everything is going to be fine!'

As far as Ben's health went, that was true enough. Over the next few days he improved steadily, staying conscious longer and responding lucidly to the nurses' questions and the doctors' probes.

He seemed willing enough to talk to them. But he didn't have much to say to Jessica.

When she came in to his room, smiling and relieved that he was aware and propped against some pillows, he looked at her warily.

'I suppose I should say thanks,' he said.

Jessica's eyes widened. 'For what?'

'Saving my life.'

Flustered, she shook her head. 'I didn't—I—'

'You did,' Ben said gruffly. 'I'd have died if you hadn't got help.'

'Well, of course I went for help!'

'So we're even now.'

Jessica stopped at the foot of the bed, trying to fathom what he was thinking. 'What do you mean?'

'I mean, go have your vacation. You destroyed my pictures, but you saved my life. Everything is square.'

'Don't be stupid! I'm not staying just because I—'

'Why *are* you staying, Jess?'

'Well, I——' she floundered '—I really felt it was my fault. If I hadn't—' She shrugged helplessly, not wanting to put into words all that had gone between them before. It didn't seem so cut-and-dried now. She wasn't quite as certain of Ben's villainy. And he had, after all, risked his neck for her, too.

'You're feeling guilty,' he said. 'Don't.'

'But—'

'I'm all right, Jessica.' His voice was almost harsh. 'I'm going to be fine.'

And he turned away from her and stared out the window, though what was so absorbing about the roofs of the cars he could see in the car park, Jessica didn't know.

She decided that it was just that he was convalescing, that he didn't like being tied down and in pain. She decided to bear with him. She just wished things were different between them.

Her wishes grew even stronger when she went back to the photographer's that afternoon to get Ben's pictures.

'How'd they turn out?' she asked the man at the photography shop.

He shook his head, grinning, marvelling. 'Amazing! Standish is the best. I've been in those woods more times than I can count, and I've never seen what he can see there. But even more than what he sees, it's the *way* he sees it that's so wonderful.' He handed Jessica the prints he had made as well as the rolls of developed film. 'He sees right to the soul of things, Standish does.' He gave her a long, penetrating look. 'He's seen right to the soul of you.'

And Jessica, looking at the photos spread out on the counter before her, knew that he had.

Ben had caught her in all her moods—sulking, unwilling, difficult, and then, amazingly enough, joyous, tender, laughing, pensive. One photo caught her with her lower lip thrust out, her hands on her hips, a glare on her face—in one of her most virulent 'anti-Ben' moods, she recognised, smiling in spite of herself. In another he had captured her sitting by the fireside, her features silhouetted in a rosy, romantic glow. There were photos of Jessica lying on the beach with her chin in her hands and of her sitting there with her head tipped back and her eyes shut, letting the sunlight kiss her face. But the one that moved her most—the one that had, in fact, seen to the depth of her soul—was one he had taken on the first night they were back in White Birch. She had been standing by the tent looking at him while he took photo after photo of everything she did. But in this one he had got under her guard and had caught her looking squarely at him, a lost, hunted and at the same time infinitely tender look on her face.

She shut her eyes against the tears that pricked behind the lids. 'Thank you,' she said. 'Thank you very much.'

'Any time.' The man gave a genial shrug. 'I don't get to work with pictures of that quality very often.'

'It doesn't come along very often,' Jessica said softly as she paid the bill and slipped the photos back into the folder he had provided.

'You're right about that.'

She went back to the hospital, subdued and chastened, knowing that Ben had put his all into these photos—just as he had into the first batch. They were wonderful, and, being wonderful, they made her feel more guilty than ever.

What if he had been telling the truth?

She carried the photos down the hall, hugging them to her chest, and wondered what Ben would say about them. No doubt he would feel vindicated, pleased. But when she got there, the room was empty.

'Where is he?' she asked the nurse at the station.

'X-ray. They're checking his ribs. He'll be back in half an hour or so.'

So Jessica sat down to wait. She leafed through the photos again. Then, because they made her want to

cry, she put them away and picked up a magazine.
She was flipping through it when the phone rang.

No one had called Ben yet that she knew of. But
now that he was national news, Gunnar might have
heard. She grimaced as she went to answer the
phone. God willing it would not be her boss. She
didn't want to have to explain to him why she was not
in Hawaii, but in Petoskey on her vacation.

'Is this Ben Standish's room?' a strong masculine
voice wanted to know.

Jessica breathed a sigh of relief. 'Yes, it is.'

'Vince Burgess here. *Preservation* magazine.'

Jessica's heartbeat quickened and she sat down
abruptly. 'Oh?'

'Is Standish all right?'

She said that he was, more or less. She told the
man about his injuries briefly, minimising them. She
didn't have to be told to know that that was the way
Ben would want it.

Burgess was sympathetic but practical. 'What
about his article?'

Her eyes fell on the photos. 'It will be there,' she
promised.

'Good. Figured I could count on him. Standish is
as reliable as the US Mail. Nothing stops him. Good
man,' he added. 'None better.'

'Really?' Jessica couldn't contain her curiosity at
this unsolicited opinion.

'Damn right,' Burgess told her. 'Ben's had a bad press. All those gossip mags.'

'You don't think he deserved it?' she asked cautiously.

'Not half of it,' he replied, matter-of-fact. 'Anyway, he's finished with all that business. Even though it would be a lot more lucrative than the wolf bit he's doing now,' he admitted.

'Are you sure he's quit? For good?' She felt the noose of false accusation tightening.

'Hell, yes, I'm sure. Last time we had lunch together I asked him about it—wanted to know why. Everybody does, I expect.'

'What did he say?'

'Said it was the stupidest thing he'd ever done.'

'But he made a lot of money at it,' Jess countered. 'He got famous, too.'

'That's just what I said,' Burgess agreed. 'But he told me it wasn't worth it. He said, "What's the use of money if you lose your soul to get it?"'

'I see,' she mumbled. And she didn't much like what she saw. Not so much about Ben, but about herself. 'I guess he had a point, Mr Burgess,' she replied, her voice shaky.

'He does indeed. Well, you tell him to get well quick, young lady. I want another article from him. Puffins on the Maine coast now. Tell him when he gets out of the hospital to give me a call.'

'I will,' she promised. She hung up and picked up the magazine again, but she didn't really see anything in it. Her mind was totally consumed with the picture of Ben that Vince Burgess had. It was the same picture that the man in the photography shop seemed to have. It was the same picture that she got herself when she looked through his photos and saw the sensitive appreciation there. It was hard to reconcile that impression with the man she had thought was going to exploit nude photos of her. She buried her head in her hands and wondered if it wasn't time to apologise to Ben for more than just causing a tree to fall on his head.

'What's the matter with you?' a gruff voice asked, and Jessica looked up to see Ben being wheeled back into the room.

She sniffed. 'N-nothing.' She tried to smile. 'A Mr Burgess just phoned from *Preservation* about your article. And I got the photos developed.'

She expected him to reach for them, to be eager to see what he had caught on film. But he wheeled the wheelchair right on past her and crawled painfully back into the bed, slumping back against the pillows, a dark look on his face.

'Don't you want to see them?' Jess asked brightly.

'Not particularly.'

'They're really good,' she continued eagerly. 'You've really caught the spirit of the place. The man in the photography shop was astounded.'

She started to take them out to show him, but he pulled the sheet over his chest as if it were a shield. 'I'm not interested, Jessica.'

She stopped and stared at him. 'But you've got to pick the ones you want to use for the article.'

'I'm not doing the article.'

'What?' she gasped.

'You heard me.' He gave her a stony stare.

'Why not?'

His look was scathing. 'I can't write, Jessica. I can't even type.'

'You could dictate it to me.'

'No.'

'Why not?'

'Why?' Ben asked bitterly. 'I don't want to.' He scowled. 'You ought to be glad. It's what you wanted, isn't it?'

'No, truly!' Jess protested. 'You should write it! I want you to!'

'More guilty conscience?' His voice was scathing.

Her face reddened. 'Yes, actually,' she admitted, ducking her head.

He snorted, then turned his face towards the wall and wouldn't speak to her again.

'I'll leave them here for you,' she said, dropping them on to the bedside table with a nonchalance she didn't feel. 'In case you change your mind.'

'I won't.'

She hoped he would.

'YOU'RE COMPLETELY out of line,' Jessica heard the floor nurse say the next day as she got off the elevator. She looked up to see the woman toe to toe with a young man, herding him backwards towards Jess. 'I don't know who you think you are, but you can leave right now, and take that—that—garbage with you!'

That 'garbage' was a video camera, a notepad, and a briefcase, all of which he was clutching against his chest as she backed him down the hall.

'You tell him.' The nurse collared Jessica. 'Mr Standish is not to be disturbed, isn't that right?'

The sandy-haired man eyed Jess curiously. 'Who are you?'

'She's Miss Mallory, Mr Standish's friend,' the nurse informed him coldly before Jessica could say a word.

Jessica herself would not have even told him her name, much less intimated that there was a relationship between herself and Ben. Long years as her mother's daughter had taught her the value of anonymity.

The man's eyes widened. 'Mallory? Daughter of...'

Jessica sighed. 'Daughter of Max Mallory, a former colleague of Mr Standish's. And the nurse is quite right, you know. He is not to be disturbed. He's—'

'Clarissa's daughter,' the man interrupted, studying her closely. 'Clarissa Evans's daughter?'

'Clarissa and Max Mallory's daughter,' Jessica said sharply. She had answered that question a million times, but still it rankled.

'Heavens,' the man muttered. His eyes bulged. She could almost see the wheels spinning in her head. 'So that's why she...' his voice trailed off and he shot an almost furtive glance down the corridor toward Ben's room.

Jessica followed his gaze, frowning. 'That's why who what?'

'Nothing.' The man gave her a quick, noncommittal smile. 'I'm Steve Harlow.' He fished in his pocket and flashed the press card from a slick national weekly magazine in front of her eyes. That made her frown even harder. 'How about just sitting down here with me then, Miss Mallory, and telling me what happened to Ben Standish.'

He was trying to manoeuvre her towards a couch in the small waiting area by the nurses' station, and the nurse, seeing that he had found another target than her patient, gave Jessica a grateful smile and vanished.

Jessica was getting annoyed. 'I really don't think he—'

'Is he going to be all right?'

'Yes. Yes, of course. He'll be fine. He—'

'How did it happen? We heard he was up north, taking photographs. Say,' he gave her a speculative look that spoke volumes, 'you weren't with him, by any chance, were you?'

Jessica folded her arms across her chest. 'Listen, Mr Harlow, I don't have to answer any of your questions. None at all.' There was one advantage to being Max's and Clarissa's daughter, she thought. She had learned years ago when not to talk to the press. And now, she decided, was definitely one of those times. 'If you'll please excuse me, I have to go now.'

'Oh, but Miss Mallory. . .'

'No, I'm sorry.' Her voice was firm and final. 'I must go.' She slipped past him and headed quickly down the hall to Ben's room, shooting the nurse heading her way a pleading glance, as if to say, 'Stop him!'

But Steve Harlow wasn't going to be easily stopped. 'Have you been in touch with your mother, Miss Mallory?'

She ignored him. She never talked about her mother. Especially not to the press. She blotted out everything he was saying, focusing her mind on the clanking of the metal supper cart that trundled down the hall, the paging of one of the doctors, the murmur of voices, one soft, one harsh, from within Ben's room.

She stopped dead just inside the door as one of those voices reached her.

'I just *had* to come,' she heard Clarissa say breathlessly.

Steve Harlow walked directly into the wall of her back.

Clarissa? Here?

Jessica caught herself against the door jamb, feeling as if he had knocked the breath right out of her. But she knew it wasn't Steve Harlow who had stunned her. It was the sight of her mother bent over Ben's bed, one long-fingered, beautifully manicured hand stroking his face. A cloud of golden hair obscured her face from Jessica's. But it didn't matter. There was no other woman on earth it could have been. And Jess had no trouble imagining how she would look to Ben. Clarissa's face would soften, and her full lips would tilt in a half-pout, half-cajoling smile.

'My poor, poor Ben!' she was saying.

'Go 'way,' Jess heard Ben snap, and he turned his head away from her so that he looked at the open door. And at Jessica.

He groaned, as if in pain.

'Hello, Mother,' Jessica said tonelessly.

That was something else she had learned early—to keep all emotion out of her voice whenever she dealt with her mother. Wherever Clarissa Evans Mallory was, the press wasn't far behind. And the press loved a scandal. So, however much Jessica would have liked to show her mother exactly how she felt at seeing her here, she wouldn't give Steve Harlow the satisfaction. Come to that, she wouldn't give it to Clarissa either.

Her mother's blonde head lifted and her blue eyes widened. The famous Clarissa Evans smile spread over her face. 'Why, Jessica darling, how wonderful to see you here!'

She *was* a good actress, Jessica thought grudgingly. Unless you knew her the way she did, you would have no idea that the words she mouthed meant no more to her than the words in her latest script. In fact, she mused, they probably meant less.

Clarissa floated across the room and bestowed a kiss on her daughter. It was an air kiss, for show only, for Steve Harlow's eyes and nothing more. 'I'm so glad to see you weren't hurt. Not like poor dear Ben.'

So much for Jessica's not telling the press anything. Steve Harlow was scribbling madly, looking from one to the other of them as if he had stumbled into a three-ring circus with all acts going at once.

Poor dear Ben looked furious. She could only guess what he was thinking if everything he had said about her mother was true. She could guess, too, the story Steve Harlow could get out of that! It was obviously up to her to do something about it. *Now*.

'I think we need to talk, Mother,' she said firmly.

It was the last thing she wanted to do. She hadn't talked to her mother more than five times in the last eight years, the last time at her father's funeral when she had had to console a broken, weeping Clarissa. It had infuriated her at the time, making her wonder how her mother could feign grief so well. But she hadn't asked her, hadn't talked to her again. She intended to talk to her now.

'Without Mr Harlow,' she added pointedly.

'Oh, but, darling, Steve is doing a story on me. He did an interview in California, took some footage at my house. But we were hoping to get a little action footage live. I just had to come when I heard about Ben. We were *soooo* close, you know.'

'Clarissa!' Ben protested sharply.

Jessica's lips tightened. 'I know.'

She avoided Ben's gaze. She did know, now. She had finally got the picture of what must have happened eight years ago straight. Ben had been telling her the truth. He was as much a victim as she had been. They had both been immature, both foolish. Both had been too young to trust that what they felt for each other was real.

And Clarissa had taken advantage of it.

Well, she was through taking advantage. Jess would see to that.

'Mother, please,' she said firmly, 'we need to talk. *Now.*'

She took Clarissa's arm. Clarissa stared at her, eyes wide and suddenly apprehensive. It was impossible to tell just what she was thinking, what she was trying to say with her eyes. But Jessica knew what she was saying with her own—that she meant to talk to her mother right now, and if Clarissa didn't agree, there would be one hell of a scene.

Clarissa got the message.

Turning her big blue eyes on Steve Harlow, batting long lashes, she said cajolingly, 'You understand how it is, Steve dear. Sometimes a mother just has to have these little talks. You'll excuse us?'

'But what about the interview? What about you and Standish?'

'You can see how weak Ben is right now,' Clarissa said as Jessica's fingers tightened on her arm. 'You go back to the hotel. We'll have dinner together. How about that?'

'Well . . .' Steve didn't look convinced.

Clarissa kissed his cheek. 'Be a good boy, Steve. I like good boys.' There was a wealth of promise in her words. Jessica felt sick.

Steve swallowed visibly. 'Don't be long.'

Clarissa ran her fingers through his hair. 'I won't be,' she said huskily.

The moment Steve had gone, she spun away from Jessica, jerking her arm free and spitting, 'Don't you *ever* grab me like that again! What do you want?'

'To talk to you. Not here.'

Clarissa considered her for a moment. Then, as if she had reflected on the history the three of them shared, she nodded. 'Where?'

'I have a motel room a few blocks away. We can go there.' Jessica turned and headed for the door.

'Jess!' Ben's voice was sharp, and she didn't want to think what he might say.

'Don't worry, I'll take care of this. Come on,' she said to Clarissa.

Neither of them spoke all the way to Jessica's motel. But when they walked in at the door of the room, Clarissa broke the silence.

'I need a drink. You don't have anything, I suppose?'

'Brandy,' Jessica remembered, thinking of the bottle the bartender had given her that sat unopened in the closet.

She fetched it and poured her mother some in one of the plastic water glasses the motel provided, then considered it solemnly and poured another glass for herself. Somehow she had never imagined sharing this particular bottle of brandy with her mother in a motel room in Petoskey, Michigan. But then how often did a person really have her life totally under control?

She carried the glasses back and handed one to her mother. Clarissa took it, lifting it in mock salute. 'To Ben.'

Jessica swirled the brandy in her glass, watching her mother take a long swallow, not touching it herself. 'What do you want with Ben?' she asked at last.

Clarissa batted the famous eyelashes. 'I think you know very well what I want, Jessica,' she purred. 'I've missed him.'

'You never had him.'

Clarissa's eyes widened, then narrowed. She took another swallow of brandy. 'Says who?' she purred.

'Ben.'

'Well, you can't expect him to tell *you* about it, darling. I mean, you are my daughter, after all.'

'Yes, I am, more's the pity. But in this case, I believe him.'

Clarissa's tongue clicked against her teeth. 'Still smitten, aren't you? Still trying to come on to the poor boy?'

'There is nothing between "the poor boy" and me, Mother,' Jessica said sharply. I destroyed that myself, she added silently.

'Well then, you shouldn't mind if I spend a little time with him.'

Her persistence surprised Jessica. She thought once her mother was sure there wasn't anything between them, she would leave him, too. 'Why?' she asked, curious in spite of herself.

'I always had a soft spot for him,' said Clarissa, and when Jessica looked doubtful, she added, 'Besides, right now he's newsworthy, and it's not easy getting in the papers any more. I need the exposure—for my career.'

'*That's* why you came here?' Jessica, even though she might have expected it, was appalled by her mother's callousness in admitting it.

'Well, you never suspected me of total altruism, did you, dear?' Clarissa mocked, lifting one incredulous brow.

Jess sighed. 'It won't do you any good, Mother. Ben won't help you this time. He doesn't need anything you have to offer. And he won't go back to Hollywood, no matter what.' It's too bad, she thought, that I didn't believe him in the first place. I could have saved us all this pain.

'He must!' Clarissa objected, shaking her head in disbelief. 'He's a wonderful photographer, the best there is.'

'As good as Walt Torberg?'

Clarissa looked as if she had been hit. 'What do you know about Walt Torberg?' she demanded.

'I know he took those pictures of you, not Ben.'

Clarissa poured another half glass of brandy for herself, tossed it down and took a deep breath. 'Ben told you.'

'Yes.' Jess found herself defending him. 'It was important,' she insisted before she realised that Clarissa didn't seem angry about it.

Her mother was staring absently into space, her mind obviously miles and years away from the tiny motel room with its shabby curtains and lumpy bed. 'It was a foolish thing to do,' she said at last, surprising Jessica. 'I see that now.'

'The pictures, you mean?' asked Jess, wanting to be sure.

'That, too,' Clarissa agreed enigmatically.

'It—it got you more parts,' Jessica offered weakly, trying to come up with some excuse for her mother's actions since Clarissa didn't seem to be offering any of her own.

'It didn't get me Max.'

Jessica stared. 'Daddy? But you already had Daddy!'

'No,' Clarissa objected sharply, 'I didn't.' She raked her long fingers through her cloud of blond hair. 'He was married to the *Adela Star*. He loved his damned fish and birds far more than he ever loved me! He loved *you* more than he loved me!'

Her hand tightened around the plastic glass, nearly cracking it. 'I wanted to shake him up,' she whispered, staring into the brandy. 'That's why I went off with Ben that way. I wanted Max to wake up, to look around and realise that he loved me, too. I wanted him to come after me.'

She gave a bitter laugh. 'Well, the joke was on me. He didn't. I don't even think he noticed I was gone. He went off to Australia and I never heard a word.'

She took another swallow of the brandy. Jessica stared at her, the revelations stunning her. Clarissa spoke again, almost to herself. 'I gave it one last shot—I let Walt Torberg take those photos. Hell, I let Walt take *me!* I needed someone to love me!' She glared at Jessica over the top of the glass, as if daring her to dispute it.

Jess just sat speechless.

'I let everyone think it was Ben because I thought that would make more of an impression on Max when he got the word. Well, the magazine got to Australia. It probably even got the Max. But he never came back.'

Jessica's mind was whirling like a kaleidoscope. Suddenly she saw whole new patterns to a reality she once thought she had completely understood.

She had never before had an inkling about how Clarissa felt, had never given a thought to what her parents' marriage had been like or what they had expected from it. She had only known what she wanted—a perfect storybook life with perfect parents—and she hadn't got it.

She realised now that her mother had nursed her own fantasy life all those years, and that it hadn't worked out any better than Jessica's did.

She felt a faint stirring of compassion, for her mother—the first, perhaps the only, she had felt in years. She was glad now that she hadn't questioned her mother's grief at Max's funeral. The grief, she suspected now, had been all too real.

'I'm sorry,' she said softly. 'I wish he'd come back to you, too.'

They looked at each other then as if they were seeing one another for the first time, each finally catching a glimpse of life in the other's world.

Clarissa's face wore an almost rueful smile. 'I'm sorry too, Jessica. About what happened all those years ago. Even,' she shrugged, 'about this.'

Jessica nodded, then stared down at the brandy in her glass. She took a swallow and felt it burn all the way down, cutting a clear path through her confusion. Her thoughts played over the past, sifting, sorting, reshuffling, then turned to the future.

'What will you do now?' she asked her mother at last.

Clarissa gave her daughter a long look, a maternal look for once. Then she shook her head, the golden halo of hair drifting around her face, enhancing her ethereal angelic beauty. 'Go home,' she replied. 'I'll leave first thing in the morning. And I'll see that Steve goes, too.'

Jessica smiled at her mother. 'Thank you.'

'You love him,' Clarissa said simply.

'Yes.'

A faint, almost wistful smile haunted Clarissa's face. 'Then I hope that at least things work out for you.'

'I do, too,' Jess said fervently.

Her mother stood up and gave her an awkward hug, then held her out at arm's length, looking her up and down. 'You'll let me know?'

'If you want.'

'I do.'

JESSICA DIDN'T sleep a wink all night. She lay awake rehearsing her apology to Ben. It was an extensive one; she had a lot to be sorry for. And each time she ran through it in her mind, she thought of something else.

By the time she arrived at the hospital, damp-palmed, dry-mouthed and apprehensive, she simply wanted to throw herself on his mercy and be done with it.

Ben, sitting in bed with a scowl on his face, didn't look in the least merciful. 'Where's your mother?' he demanded.

'She left.'

'Didn't she think I'd help her image this time? Too many bruises?' he asked sarcastically.

'She realised what she was going to do was wrong.'

'I suppose she's on a guilt trip now, too.'

Jess took a steadying breath. 'I don't know how *she* feels. I only know how I feel, and I feel terrible.'

Ben stared at her wordlessly, his expression hard.

She could have done with some encouragement, Jessica thought. But Ben looked less interested than the Sphinx in giving her any. Her looked bored in fact, as if nothing she had to say interested him at all. But, gripping the rail at the foot of the bed, she plunged on. 'I was wrong, Ben. I'm sorry. I—'

'Forget it, Jessica.'

'I can't forget. I want to apologise. I want...I love you!'

He wasn't bored any longer. His eyes glittered angrily. 'Sure you do,' he said scornfully. 'Well, you had a damned funny way of showing it!'

'I know, Ben. I'm sorry. Please, what can I say? What can I do?'

His jaw clenched. 'Leave.'

She stared, disbelieving. 'Leave? What do you mean?'

'I mean that I want you to walk out that door and don't come back. I mean get out of my life—just like your mother!'

'Ben, I love you!'

He gave a harsh laugh. 'If you'd loved me, Jess, you'd have trusted me. If you'd loved me, I wouldn't be sitting here now.'

Jessica's shoulders sagged. He was right, of course. 'I'm sorry,' she whispered.

'Me too,' he said, but his voice was implacable. They stared at each other, until her eyes finally dropped.

'Just go, Jessica,' he said finally. 'And—' he tossed the packet of photos and negatives at her '—take these damned things with you. I don't ever want to see them—or you—again!'

CHAPTER ELEVEN

GUNNAR HALVORSEN was ecstatic, and Jessica supposed she couldn't blame him. The White Birch Bay coverage in the October issue of *Preservation* was even more impressive than she had hoped. But she still couldn't help wincing when he waved her advance copy in her face and said, 'See? I knew Standish would do well by us! These photos are first-rate, and the article is outstanding. He really must have picked your brains, my dear. He seems to know wolves inside out.'

'Mmm.' Jessica nodded, not trusting herself to look up from the monograph she was reading, and not about to tell Gunnar that she was the person who had written that 'outstanding' text. Ever since she had sent it off to Vince Burgess, she had tried to forget about it—to forget about Ben—and seeing it now was so painful that she realised she wasn't close to getting over him yet.

She had written the article as soon as she came back to Madison, the day after Ben had tossed both her and his photos out of his hospital room. It was a point of honour, she decided. Though Ben would no doubt consider it even more self-serving behaviour on her part and be angrier with her than ever. But she knew she wasn't doing it for that.

She was doing it because the pictures Ben took were too wonderful to be wasted. And regardless of what had happened between them, a commitment to the article had been made. Vince Burgess and his magazine shouldn't have to suffer for her sins and Ben's. Besides, if she were truly going to be a 'professional', as Ben had so often mocked her for trying to be, then she was obliged to do the article. It was as simple as that.

It would be a cathartic experience. At least that was what she had told herself. By re-living it all one last time, she thought she could get Ben out of her system, convince herself that it didn't really matter that he wanted nothing more to do with her, and that some day she would find another man to love and share her life with.

It didn't work.

She sloughed through the days and stared at the ceiling through the nights, always remembering Ben and the love she had lost. She told herself that things would get better, too. And now Gunnar had proved her wrong there as well. It had been six weeks, three days and twelve hours since she had seen Ben, and 'better' hadn't even begun yet.

In fact as the day wore on, things just got worse. Gunnar had gone around chortling, his eyes alight with the prospect of increased funds due to all this wonderful publicity. And Geri, whose comments about Jessica and her weeks in the woods with Ben Standish had begun to taper off after several weeks of non-response from Jessica, started right in speculating again.

'He sure captured the real you,' she said, studying the pictures of Jess that Vince Burgess had selected to accompany Jess's text. Geri raised her eyes and considered Jessica closely. 'Are you certain nothing happened between you two?'

'Nothing important,' lied Jess, keeping her eyes firmly on the deathless prose of the monograph on salmon migration that she was trying to read.

'Still the Ice Princess, huh?' asked Matt, smiling as if he were almost satisfied with the idea that even the notorious Ben Standish hadn't been able to thaw Jessica Mallory either.

If only you knew, Jess thought grimly.

She shut the monograph and stood up. 'Still an Ice Princess,' she assured him drily. Then, glancing at her watch, she told Gunnar, 'I have a dentist's appointment. I'll have to leave now, OK?'

'Sure, fine. Say, can I borrow the article overnight? I want to show my wife.'

'Be my guest.' Keep it, she wanted to say. It had
hurt her more than she would have believed possible. The only thing worse than not seeing Ben, she
discovered, was seeing photographs he had taken. It
was painful to think how far she still had to go to get
over him.

The dentist's office was just the right sort of place
to have to spend the rest of the afternoon. It suited
her mood exactly. When she left there, she found
herself wishing that her feelings were as numb as her
mouth was. But regardless of how many days it had
been, she still ached over the loss of Ben. Today, because of the article, was worse than most. And when
she thought about the long lonely evening ahead, she
cast about to try to come up with some other er-
rands that would keep her out and about for a while.
She stopped to fill the tank with gasoline, then went
for a walk along the shore of Lake Mendota, then
stopped to buy groceries and a birthday card for her
mother.

She and Clarissa were communicating still. Perhaps, Jess thought, it was because they had both
loved and lost. But her mother was showing some
real interest in her for a change, trying to pick up the
pieces of a relationship that had crumbled years before. And after Jessica had reluctantly reported that
Ben wanted nothing to do with her, Clarissa had even
had the good sense not to tell her that she would get

over it. She had said simply, 'I'm sorry,' and Jessica believed she really was.

The card chosen, the car full of fuel and the groceries purchased, Jessica could think of nothing else to keep her from going home. But she still took her time, concentrating on the beauty of the crisp autumn afternoons as she parked the car and locked it, then hoisted the grocery bag on to her hip and walking towards the stairs to her apartment.

She bent to pet Mrs Franco's cat which wove between her legs as she started up the steps. Mrs Franco's curtains twitched as Jessica neared the top and she smiled at them almost ruefully.

Mrs Franco hadn't twitched her curtains in ages. There had been no one to twitch her curtains *at*. Not a single person 'of the male persuasion', as Mrs Franco would say, had come or gone at Jessica's since that fateful evening when Ben and Kyle had both arrived.

Jess was about to sing out, 'Sorry, Mrs Franco,' when she turned at the top step and heard a low, achingly familiar voice say,

'About time.' And the grocery sack was lifted from her arms.

'Ben!'

She spun around, disbelieving, to stare up into his eyes.

Then, 'Ben?' she said again, more hesitantly this time, not at all sure what his presence on her doorstep meant. Surely he couldn't have been so angry at her writing the article that he had dropped everything and rushed to Madison to chew her out. Had he?

'I wonder,' said Ben, 'if you could invite me in.' He glanced pointedly at Mrs Franco's window. 'Some lady has been staring at me through those curtains for hours.'

Hours? Jess tried to digest that. How long had he been there, for goodness sake?

And why, oh, why had he come?

She wanted to hope, but she couldn't. Her hopes had been dashed too many times. She couldn't lift them again, only to watch them be shattered once more.

But, oh, he looked gorgeous! To her eyes, at least. She supposed, from a purely medical standpoint, he looked weary, thin, and like a man who had travelled a very long road to recovery.

But recover he obviously had. His arm was out of the cast, although he held it carefully at his side while with his other arm he cradled her groceries. His bruises had all vanished. But there were new lines around his eyes, and the grooves scoring his cheeks were deeper now. She wanted to touch them—touch him. But she didn't dare.

Instead she fumbled with her keys, opened the door and stepped back to let him pass. Looking over her shoulder as she followed him in, she saw the curtains twitch once more for good measure.

She crossed her fingers.

Ben set the grocery sack on the counter and stood looking at her, not speaking. Not showing the slightest emotion in those wolf's eyes of his.

Jessica licked her lips. 'You—you look wonderful,' she said at last, awkwardly.

'Thanks to you.'

She felt the heat rise in her cheeks. 'Hardly. I mean, it was my fault you were—that you were even—I mean, I—' She floundered miserably and twisted her fingers together in despair.

Ben reached out and touched her chin, lifting it so that she was forced to look up into his hazel eyes. 'I think we could fight about who owns most of the blame forever, Jess. I don't want to do that.'

She swallowed hard, groping behind her for the support of the wall, a chair, anything to shore up her suddenly quaking knees. 'What do you want?' she whispered.

'You.'

One simple word and he took her breath away.

She stared at him, heart hammering.

He met her eyes for a moment, then ran his hand beneath his shirt collar as he sighed and dropped his gaze. 'Is it too late?' he asked, his voice rough and slightly unsteady.

'Too late?'

He rammed his fists into the pockets of his jeans, then lifted his eyes to face her squarely. 'Too late to say I'm sorry. Too late to ask you to try again, to make things work for us this time. Damn it, Jess, I love you! And you have every right to hate my guts after the way I treated you at the hospital.' She saw a flicker of apprehension in his eyes. 'Do you?'

But Jessica didn't even hear the question. All she heard were the three words that mattered most to her in the world. 'You love me?' she echoed, amazed.

'Lord, yes, I love you!'

'Then—' anguished '—then *why* did you tell me to go away?'

Ben raked his fingers through his hair. 'Because I was angry. Because I felt I'd been betrayed. Because I thought you loved me the first time when we were at White Birch Bay, and then you threw everything back in my face!'

'I did love you,' she assured him fervently. 'It was just that I didn't know! I thought you and my mother had—I know you said she had asked you... but for eight years I believed otherwise. And I thought you took those pictures, Ben! I never knew! She never said!'

'I know.' Ben pulled her against him, wrapping strong arms around her and hugging her close. 'I know. She told me.'

Jess pulled back, astonished. 'Clarissa told you?'

A faint grin quirked one corner of his mouth. 'Uh-huh. In fact, I guess you could credit Clarissa with me being here today.'

That did make Jessica's jaw drop. 'What do you mean?'

'I got discharged from the hospital last month, and I went back to Missouri to lick my wounds, so to speak. I was still madder than hell at you. I told myself I could get over you, that I could go on and just forget about loving you. But I couldn't.'

His rueful smile told her that he had suffered through exactly the same pain she had. She lifted her arms around his neck and linked her fingers together, pulling his head down and touching her lips to his. 'I know just what you mean.'

'Do you?' He looked doubtful. Then, seeing his pain mirrored in her eyes, he nodded slowly. 'Yeah, I guess maybe you do. Clarissa said you were hurting.'

She tugged the hair at the nape of his neck. 'What does Clarissa have to do with this? When did you talk to her?'

'She came to Missouri.'

'She didn't!'

Ben nodded, grinning. 'I was hung over, still angry, and I'd just spoiled an entire roll of film doing something so stupid that even a rank amateur would have known better. Shows just how bad off I was. In fact, I was considering putting my fist right through a window when I saw her standing on the other side of it.' He laughed, shaking his head. 'Lord, I thought I was hallucinating!'

'You weren't?'

'Nope. She came in, sobered me up on gallons of black coffee and a ton of maternal advice.' He grinned. 'I never thought Clarissa had that much maternal instinct in her.'

'What did she say?' demanded Jessica, her mind spinning at the thought of Clarissa playing matchmaker.

'That I was a fool.' He gave a wry grin. 'She said that if two people were apart because one of them didn't care—as Max apparently didn't care about her enough to fight for her—well, that was one thing. But if they both loved each other and they were just too stubborn to try to work things out, that was different. Then she asked me if I loved you.'

'And?'

He sighed. 'And I said, "I don't want to, but I do." And she said, "Odd. Jessica said the same thing about you."' He shook his head, as if recalling just how astonished he had felt. 'I didn't believe her.'

'But why not? You must have seen the way I hung about you at the hospital. I positively hovered. I even told you that I loved you!'

'Guilt,' Ben explained. 'I thought you just felt sorry for me. I thought you were hanging around because you'd got me into that fix because of the photographs. And that made me madder than ever! I didn't want you that way, for heaven's sake!

'I loved you,' Jess told him, her voice firm. 'I couldn't help myself. Even when I thought I hated you—after I saw those pictures you took—I still couldn't stop loving you. You are in my blood, a part of me.' She rested her head against his shoulder. 'While you were in the hospital I found out that my love was justified and my hatred wasn't. I got a lot of other people's opinions of you—all unsolicited. The man in the photography shop who developed the pictures, Vince Burgess, my mother. And every one of them made me realise that I had misjudged you.' She lifted her head and looked up at him. 'They made me see how wrong I'd been, and how badly I had treated you. I don't blame you for sending me away.'

Ben drew her down on the couch, putting his arms around her, holding her against his heart. 'I was wrong to do it. But I was hurt,' he told her softly, brushing his lips against her hair. 'Just the way you were when you saw the pictures. I lashed out, just the way you did. But I couldn't stop loving you either.'

'Thank God,' Jess murmured. 'I love you,' she told him. Then wanting to be absolutely sure he understood, she said it again. 'I love you with all my heart.'

He kissed her then, the way she had always wanted to be kissed, with a slow, aching thoroughness that drew warmth and love from her as he shared with her his own. Then he sighed and pulled back a little, resting his head on the back of the couch, closing his eyes. 'God bless Clarissa,' he muttered.

'Amen,' she concurred, then laughed. 'I hope she'll be pleased.'

'She will.'

'I'm glad.' Jessica sent a prayer of thanks to her mother, wishing that Clarissa's love story had worked out as well as hers.

'But it wasn't just Clarissa,' Ben told her. 'It was your doing, too.'

'How?'

'That article you wrote for Vince.' He pulled a copy out of the pocket of the cotton jacket he wore, waving it beneath her nose. 'When I saw it I began to believe Clarissa was right. I wanted to believe you had done it for me, for us. Did you?'

'Oh, yes.'

He smiled. 'It was terrific! And although I suppose I ought to be wary of taking credit for someone else's work after what happened with Walt's photos of Clarissa, this time I think I will.' He bent his head and kissed her on the lips. 'I like to think it's what I would have written if I'd been thinking straight.'

He unfolded the article, scanning down the last page until he found the passage he was looking for. '"We admired the wolves' love and their commitment to each other,"' he quoted. '"Time and distance might keep them apart, but ultimately the bonds between them bring them together again. It is a lesson we humans could learn as well." I hope now that I've learned *my* lesson.' He touched his lips to her hair, then kissed her ear, making her shiver.

She lifted up, snuggling closer to him, kissing him back, savouring the man and the love he shared with her. 'There's a lesson in every expedition,' she told him, smiling. 'That's what Max always said.'

'And it's not always what you'd expect,' Ben grinned.

'No. What did you expect?' she asked him. 'When you found out it was me, I mean.'

'I didn't know what to expect,' said Ben, his expression serious. 'I couldn't figure it. I mean, one minute I was going on a routine assignment with that Morrow guy, and the next thing I know I get a note saying he's been replaced, followed by a terse little memo from J.D. Mallory.' He grinned, remembering. 'I was intrigued. Mallory is a name that means a lot to me.'

'I'll bet,' Jessica said, grimacing.

'When I found out it was you I had mixed feelings. I remembered the chemistry between us, of course. Who wouldn't? Nothing like it had ever happened to me before—or since. But I wasn't sure how you felt. I guess I was hoping that if you chose to come along it was because you still thought you were attracted to me. It wasn't, I gather?' he added drily.

'No. The opposite in fact. I thought I hated you. But—' and she just realised this then herself '—I think unconsciously I must have measured every man I ever went out with against you, against what I felt for you.'

'How'd they measure up?'

She kissed his chin. 'They didn't.'

'No one ever measured up to you either, Jess. I have loved you since I first knew you eight years ago. I fought against it then. I thought you were too young. I thought we couldn't make it last and that I could go on with my life and meet someone else who would mean just as much to me. But I didn't understand then what I understand now. I won't ever get over you, Jess. You are my only woman.' He kissed her soundly. 'Will you marry me?'

Jessica, having waited for those words for eight long years, hugged him tightly. 'You don't know how many times I've already said yes!'

'Thank God,' he murmured, and turned her, bearing her back against the couch, beginning to love her in the way she had feared she would never be loved again.

Blinking back tears of joy, she moved to love him, too. Their fingers fumbled with buttons and zippers, their touches at once shy and desperate. Soft light filtered into the room as the evening sun peeped out from behind a passing cloud. A gust of cool autumn air brushed across their hot bodies through the barely open window.

But it wasn't the feel of the wind against her damp skin that made Jess shiver. It was the look of love on Ben's face and the touch of his trembling hands as they skimmed her clothes aside and reverently caressed her body.

She reached for him, drawing him down off the narrow couch and on to the thick carpet.

'Here?' Amusement flickered in Ben's eyes, although he dropped willingly beside her.

Jessica put arms around him, sliding them up the smooth-muscled expanse of his back. 'Here,' she declared. 'It's not quite the forest primeval, but it is green.'

'And there aren't any mosquitoes,' said Ben, smiling as he settled himself between her thighs.

'That, too,' Jess murmured against his lips. 'A definite plus.'

She drew him into her waiting warmth and softness, and she could tell at once from the look on his face that mosquitoes had entirely slipped his mind. 'It has all sorts of advantages,' she whispered.

He began to move, his eyes glittering darkly, his face taut with passion. 'It does,' he groaned thickly. 'Oh God, yes, Jess. It does!'

AFTERWARDS he couldn't stop touching her.

They lay side by side on the carpet, and Ben propped himself up on one elbow while his other hand skimmed lightly down her leg then travelled up her body again and stroked the damp tendrils of hair away from her face.

'You are beautiful,' he told her, looking deeply into her eyes, his expression serious, penetrating. 'That's the only reason I took those pictures, Jess. I went for a walk the morning after we made love the first time. I needed to think. And when I got back, I saw you swimming in the lake. You were exquisite. I couldn't stop looking at you. And I wanted to capture you just the way you were then, because that's when I knew for certain that I was in love with you. But I didn't know yet how you felt. Do you understand?' Doubt and hope mingled in his look of entreaty.

'I understand,' said Jess, stroking his cheek. 'I know that now.'

Ben smiled. 'Good.'

He got to his feet, then lifted her into his arms, walking with her toward her open bedroom door.

'Where are we going?' she asked him, smiling up into his eyes.

'To bed,' he told her. 'If we really are going to learn a lesson from those wolves of yours and become loving, committed spouses for all eternity, then I want the whole works.'

He carried her into the bedroom and set her gently on to the springy mattress, then dropped down beside her and wrapped her in his arms once more. 'I want to work some more on starting our very own pack!'